Circle of Deception

CIRCLE OF DECEPTION

★ ★ ★ ★ ★ ★ ★

Roger Elwood

 Tyndale House Publishers, Inc.
Wheaton, Illinois

Library of Congress Cataloging-in-Publication Data
Elwood. Roger.
  Circle of deception / Roger Elwood
    p.   cm.
  ISBN 0-8423-1128-9
  I. Title
PS355.L85C57 1993
813'.54—dc20   93-19262

Printed in the United States of America

99 98 97 96 95 94 93
9   8   7   6   5   4   3   2   1

To Bill and Ken Petersen—
prime movers
★ ★ ★

Acknowledgments

★ ★ ★

Not every editor is a writer, and not every writer is an editor. I have been both, and the experiences the Lord has given me on both sides of the desk have been invaluable.

So it is with Ken Petersen. He is an editor, he is a writer, he understands both temperaments—and he is one of the three best editors with whom I have worked over a period of twenty-eight years.

But there are others presently at Tyndale House or retired therefrom to whom I owe a debt. One is Ron Beers, and I thank him heartily. The other is Dwight Hooten, editor emeritus of the *Christian Reader,* and the sort of friend-supporter with whom one is blessed only rarely in a lifetime.

Roger Elwood

Ephesians 6:12 puts the facts on the table: "For we wrestle not against flesh and blood, but against principalities, against powers, against the rulers of the darkness of this world, against spiritual wickedness in high places."

While the real enemies today are not "flesh and blood," as Scripture tells us, which means they are demonic entities empowered by Satan to cause havoc through a world that was once a place of purity and beauty before Adam and Eve sinned, these perverse spiritual creatures often use mortal puppets, human beings through whom they work, to bring about the dark and unholy circumstances to which they are dedicated.

Much of *Circle of Deception* is based upon this single compelling verse and yet, also, upon what the totality of God's Word tells us about human nature, about the sin nature that makes us do, as the apostle Paul has admitted in his own case, that which we know we should not and avoid doing that which we should. When we should be acting as Christians and serve as proper witnesses to the unsaved world around us, we tend to negate our testimony by being an embarrassment to our Lord instead of a beacon.

That phrase "spiritual wickedness in high places" delineates a phenomenon that will characterize the so-called "end times." It puts the lie to humanistic contentions that if people are left alone, they will elevate themselves to a higher moral plane.

But the average Christian is basically uninformed about just how widespread this spiritual wickedness is within the manifold governments of the world. Oh, they are generally aware of the political scandal of the moment, whether Watergate, Irangate,

Iraqgate, or whatever the current tempest happens to be. But these tend to come and go, rather like hula hoops and miniskirts and the rest, pungent at the time but soon forgotten.

Yet there is a dark, sinister influence that does remain, with a continuing wave of people in subjection to vile passions, even after the current uproar dies down, because what we hear about is not the whole story. The crew of the *Titanic* failed to see the rest of the iceberg, and their ship sank as a result.

That is not an inappropriate analogy, you know. The Watergates of our recent history reveal only the most obvious crimes, leaving us complacent when the criminals themselves are apprehended, for we tend to think that the cancer has been eradicated, and yet it is, in this case, only in remission at best.

Circle of Deception is a work of fiction. But it brings together a number of various threads of devastating facts, facts that seem bizarre and melodramatic.

Not so.

A key plot element in *Circle of Deception* is taken up with Operation Paperclip. This is not a fictitious name nor has the conduct of the U.S. government it details been exaggerated for dramatic effect.

Secret Agenda, which was written by Linda Hunt and published by St. Martin's Press, is a fascinating *nonfiction* work that deals entirely with "Paperclip." *Dirty Little Secrets,* written by James F. Dunnigan and Albert A. Nofi, and published by William Morrow and Company reads like an encyclopedia of governmental manipulation of the truth. This is joined by *Hitler's Undercover War* by William Breuer, also from St. Martin's Press, and, frankly, a number of other sources, including *Time* magazine, various newspapers such as the *Los Angeles Times,* and, arrestingly, the "60 Minutes" television program.

The latter featured an episode dealing with the Tuskegee Project, which is a prominent part of *Circle of Deception*.

We live in a world that evidences the tightening grip of the Arch Deceiver—the Prince of Lies—Satan himself. Even the most well-versed in matters of prophecy may be taken aback by the *devices* Satan will use and the *avenues* he intends to travel as he tries to implement his battle plan against all that is righteous.

Circle of Deception incorporates a number of not generally known but nonetheless documented facts, designed to show in fictional terms how Satan can use the governments of this world for his diabolical purposes.

As you read *Circle of Deception*, realize that it reflects more than just one author's creative imagination. It is the result of that, yes, but also the insights of many individuals who have been consulted about the possibilities herein and have given their views and information against a backdrop of the greatest possibility of all—that what we read in newspapers and magazines, and glean from television newscasts in terms of "wickedness in high places," is but a reminder of that which the holy Word of God proclaims in verse after verse—namely, that an apocalyptic end awaits human civilization *as we know it now,* this climax to history being part of God's divine plan for the ages, which may be playing itself out at this very moment.

1

★ ★ ★

"Nick's body finally has been discovered, Mrs. Tazelaar. He was brutally tortured before his death. . . ."

Heather Tazelaar could not be content with the explanation being given for her husband's death, for it was meant very efficiently to tie together all loose ends, including on whom to place the blame, and in the process leaving nothing to question, yet she had learned from Nick that in his unholy business answers were never quite so simple to come by.

"It's a business of the most damnable lies, lies that are sometimes capable of changing the course of history on this planet, at least from mankind's point of view," he would tell her. *"Deception is at the heart of everything. I've learned to believe only 10 percent of what anyone tells me. That's how I have to work, Heather. That's what I must face every day. It's why our marriage is my salvation. It's the one aspect of my life that I can depend on being completely honest."*

Despite her misgivings, she tried to be polite, tried to pretend to the tall, rather handsome young man who sat on the sofa opposite her chair that what he was saying, what this Karl-somebody would

1

like to have her swallow, so totally went beyond the "official" story and was actually the truth.

. . . beyond the "official" story and was actually the truth.

Initially, there was no reason to suspect otherwise, especially when he showed her the photographs of Nick's body.

In a storm drain on the outskirts of dreary Düsseldorf, Germany. He looked like a rag doll that had been contemptuously tossed aside, now distorted by death and barely recognizable, the hair turned white, the skin wrinkled and splotched like that of a much older man, because of whatever unspeakable acts his captors had inflicted upon him; his countenance was indeed so abused that a decision for the sake of her emotional stability was made by strangers to keep the coffin sealed, for few who knew him well would be able to endure the shock of seeing what he had become.

Düsseldorf!

How Nick had hated that city, almost as strongly as he felt about Hamburg. It was everything cold and inhuman that had ever arisen in the brutal German past. He was always glad to leave what seemed a bit like hell to him.

"He was dumped there quite some time ago. First, Nick was tortured, then, well, it is as you can see."

Those were not the words that this Karl-somebody used. He tried to be more discreet, tried to talk to her with some sensitivity about her feelings, but when all the politeness was stripped away, she knew that that was the essence of what had happened to someone she loved so very much.

Heather leafed through the shots, saw familiar clothes, a watch, his wedding ring, a burgundy eel-skin wallet, other items, all of them fortifying the contention that it was indeed Nick's lifeless, long-cold, abused body.

"His face," she said, her voice trembling for a moment despite her determination to hold back, to be outwardly strong, "there's nothing . . . left."

"Acid," Karl-somebody remarked.

Heather handed the photos back to him.

"He was so good at what he did," she remarked wistfully. "I suppose I convinced myself that nothing like this would ever happen to Nick. My husband was just too smart, too experienced to be trapped as he must have been for any of this ever to have taken place."

"But hardly infallible, I might add, ma'am. Nick Tazelaar could escape 999 times but then that final one, the thousandth, it was apparently enough to bring about what you have seen."

"But why so thorough?" she asked. "There's no way to recognize him. Is that what they wanted, for no one to be able to say just who it was?"

"I can't tell you that," Karl-somebody replied. "They left his teeth intact, and his fingerprints. So they were either very sloppy, or disguise wasn't what they had in mind. It may have been for spite."

"Out of *revenge*? Is that what you're saying?"

"Possibly, ma'am. Your husband cost them a great deal of money. They had to express their anger in some dramatic, visible way, as a warning that no one should interfere again. That's why the job of obliterating—"

His face flushed red. "Sorry," he said. "That was pretty insensitive of me."

She brushed aside his embarrassment with a wave of her hand.

"Has it worked?" Heather asked.

"I don't know what you mean."

"*Are* you going to go easy on these people?"

3

"Of course not! We can never reward gunrunners or others of their ilk for this kind of intimidation. They'll regret ever murdering Nick. I for one can promise you that, Mrs. Tazelaar."

The man gave Heather a stock smile, shook her hand limply, and then indicated that he must leave, as though glad to be able to extricate himself from facing her any longer.

"It's been a bad month," he admitted emotionlessly. "Four other agents are dead, you know. You heard, of course, of the two gunned down right in front of headquarters."

"Any connection with my husband's murder?"

"Impossible to tell at this stage," he replied in a manner that spoke of rehearsal in response to such a question.

Heather was glad to see Karl-somebody go. She stood in the doorway, watching him get into the car he had parked out front then drive off.

I don't like this man, she thought, ashamed of herself for making such a snap judgment but nevertheless unable to stop from doing so. *I don't trust him at all. And I surely don't believe him.*

As she turned back into the house, the images of that body in that dreary place in the photos stayed with her.

He shows me some almost formless heap, shot from different angles, and expects me just to accept it as . . . Nick.

Suddenly Heather cried out in that large and suffocatingly empty house of theirs, devastated by the knowledge that Nick had been physically abused with such intensity before he died that there was not much left of his face or his hands. While she was surrounded by every convenience, and living comfortably, Nick must have been suffering the greatest agony.

Darling, the pain . . . the awful pain! If only I could have shared it with you, helped you through it! But I wasn't able to be there for you. I wasn't—

And then her grief, no longer able to be contained by the responsibilities of the funeral and social propriety, flooded through her in wave after wave.

Nick, Nick, I didn't get to say good-bye.

Without question, that was the worst part of what had happened—not to be by Nick's side, not to touch his familiar hand nor whisper some earnest prayer of love and faith and heavenly reunion into his ear before that hand grew limp and he was gone.

Oh, Nick, if only I could have held you one more time, if I could have—

But she was not able to finish that thought, those words. She could not because, all at once, she realized that there might be no lies involved, that Karl-somebody could have been telling the truth, and what she would be standing next to in three days was a closed coffin that did, in fact, contain Nick's body, though she would have to take the word of nameless strangers that this was so.

After a few minutes, she walked numbly to their bedroom, stopped for a moment before a full-length mirror attached to their large closet.

Early forties, red-haired, round-faced, with just a hint of freckles, still lean, with a figure reminiscent of her college years. I shouldn't be ready so soon, Lord, not ready to give up on life, not the way I look even now, in the midst of this awful pain. Yet I wonder, oh, Jesus, I wonder if there is anything left for me, anything at all.

Heather turned from the mirror and walked over to the foot of the familiar canopied, frill-fringed bed, memories of lovemaking as well as moments of just sitting back and talking returning as fresh as ever to her—beautiful times when they shared their bodies, their minds, everything intimate and personal that they could with one another.

There was nothing I didn't know about you, she thought, her heartbeat accelerating. *There was nothing I ever held back from you, ever wanted to. We merged, Nick, we merged beyond anything physical.*

Heather sat on the edge of the bed, panning the blue-hued room—light blue, her favorite color but not Nick's, and yet that didn't matter to him, for he gave her whatever she wanted, and knowing this, she asked for little.

Dear Jesus, how can I do this? Lord, how can I go on in life without this man, this blessed man?

She fell back on the bed, sobbing, and, after a short while, lapsed into something resembling sleep.

He was a large man, fat bulging around his belly, though he generally tried to deceive anyone who would listen into thinking that it was solid muscle instead. Large, yes, and more than a hundred pounds too heavy, but he paid attention to his clothes, each suit hand-tailored, hand-painted silk ties, his shirts silk from Oxford Street, his shoes high-grade leather from Italy, his cigars hand-rolled through a special arrangement with "contacts" just outside Havana, Cuba.

The clouds of smoke were onerous to visitors, but no one complained, no one dared say anything about the smelly stuff because that would irritate this fat man, and while he would seem to take it all in good spirits, he would be plotting a more indelicate response behind that artificial smile on that overstuffed face, with its bulldog jowls.

The leather-surfaced chair that held him creaked with protest as he leaned forward and tapped the fingers of his left hand impatiently on the hand-rubbed teak top of a desk that had been crafted directly for him.

"You sure?" he asked bluntly, little spitlets of saliva drooling out of the sides of a mouth that seemed to be pulled permanently in the direction of that cigar, making his puffy lips seem all the more repulsive.

The young man sitting in a chair in front of the desk nodded. "One to go," he said, trying to force a smile, but failing under the circumstances, which made him an actor with an audience of one as he tried to appear confident and relaxed before someone who could have him castrated within the next five minutes if he became a source of the slightest displeasure.

"How soon?" the fat one asked. "Tell me that."

"It took a year or two for the others," the other pointed out. "If we step up the schedule, it could raise some eyebrows, some questions."

"If we wait too long, the remaining one could become a very lethal dagger aimed at our throats."

To emphasize that point, he took a large dagger-cum-letter-opener out of the center drawer of the desk and a pencil from a round holder to his right. In an instant he had chopped the pencil in half.

"It is so easy to separate a head from a neck," he went on. "I don't intend to give anyone, FBI agent or whoever else, the remotest opportunity for anything of the sort—in my case, that is. If anything like that is going to happen, I promise you that *I* shall be the one to use the dagger, *understand?*"

"I see your point, sir," the young man replied lamely.

"Now *that* encourages me," the fat one said, laughing coldly, his voice filled with nerve-jarring harshness. "I shall sleep well tonight knowing that this 'caper,' shall we call it, is in such capable hands."

His eyes narrowed to the extent of being little more than creases in an expanse of lard.

"Nick Tazelaar," he said, savoring the name. "He was the most important. I'm almost sorry we never met. The other put up a fight, but he was no match for us. This last one, I predict, will be far easier to deal with."

The young man breathed a too-sudden, too-exuberant sigh of relief.

"I did not say easy!" the fat one bellowed, his face turning red. "Do you understand or *don't* you?"

"I do," the other told him, determined not to show any emotion, anxiety, uncertainty, anger, whatever, and he thought he had succeeded.

"You're sweating."

That statement was an observation but also an accusation.

"I suppose I'm a little warm, Mr. Stelzfuss," the young one said, trying to camouflage the real cause.

"It's cooler than usual in here," Stelzfuss said.

"Perhaps you're right."

"But I still see beads of sweat on your forehead. Ah, several have merged, and formed a little trickle down your left cheek."

He jerked the long, dark cigar out of his mouth and slammed it down into an black marble ashtray.

The young man was expecting something quite awful. Erik Stelzfuss was angry, was angry at him!

"You're dismissed," Stelzfuss said suddenly. "Keep me posted."

The young man nodded, stood, and hurried out of that office, stuffed as it was with the accumulated souvenirs of a madman, rifles and pistols and serrated knives that spoke much of the personality of the one who acquired them—in the background, chuckles following his hasty exit like a devil bat from the pit of hell.

Erik Stelzfuss did enjoy toying with the young, handsome ones. It had to do with their relative innocence, taking it in his massive hands, and squeezing the life out of it, until what was left was a conscienceless puppet whose strings he managed to control twenty-four hours a day.

His kind once scoffed at me, speaking to me with sarcasm that every single one came to regret, Stelzfuss thought as the door closed, and he was left alone. *So young they were, so strong.*

None dared mock him anymore. That was one basic reason why he relished the power that had come his way over the years, accumulated through whatever means he found necessary. With it, he could eliminate from his life those who attempted to degrade him by their scorn.

I can wipe any such pitying, demeaning smiles or sneers away in an instant, along with the face itself.

His body shook with anger.

Even as I sense that there are those who would dare to plot against me.

He glanced at a photo of the thirty-fifth president of the United States.

"Someday, perhaps," he said out loud, a sneer in his voice, "they will realize how foolish they are."

2

★ ★ ★

Noon. Forest Lawn Memorial Park.

The air was clear, warmish that day, the sky free of its typical smog overlay, the scent of flowers drifting across that knoll. Birds were singing from a row of nearby trees. Butterflies floated over several of the long line of limousines that clogged the driveway.

Nothing less would have been appropriate for Nick Tazelaar. His employer insisted upon paying for everything.

His employer. . . .

Heather Tazelaar looked at the nearly fifty men and women who stood around her husband's closed cherry wood coffin. She recognized only two: Lloyd Brahill, who was Nick's attorney, along with Melody, Brahill's wife.

How many of these people work for the ever-present agency? How many are like my beloved Nick, seeing where they might well end up someday, not from natural causes but through an act of violence by criminals fighting back? How many are shedding tears, not for Nick but for themselves, their loved ones? How many are counteragents, working for the other side, whatever that side is these days? Oh Lord, never has it been more necessary to feel Thy presence with me. I cannot go on without Thee by my side. I am not strong enough or wise enough to do it alone, dear Jesus!

She had insisted upon remaining behind, in order to watch the heavy coffin being lowered into her husband's grave. By then only a handful of the mourners remained. One of these was her next-door neighbor, cute but overweight Rebecca Huizinga, who stood beside her, an ample arm around her waist, to keep her from falling.

"You know, don't you?" Heather remarked appreciatively.

"About what it's like?"

"Yes. It was the same for Douglas, wasn't it?"

"Not completely, Heather. No body was found. At least you know that that is Nick's in there."

She was pointing to the coffin as she spoke, remembering her own husband's funeral, remembering the empty one that was used.

"Do I, Becky?" Heather replied. "Can I really say that it *is* Nick?"

Rebecca looked at her oddly.

"Why in the world would you doubt that?" she asked.

"Because I can't *see* him, I can't hold him, I can't decide for myself that he's there, the physical shell is there. That was taken away from me, that final contact. It tears at me, Becky. You can't imagine how much it hurts."

As soon as she said that, she regretted it, for her friend surely did know the anguish caused by having *no one* to touch, to kiss, to say good-bye to except through whatever memories she could conjure up in her mind.

"Forgive me, Becky," she said, voice trembling.

"No need to ask. We share the same abyss."

Becky Huizinga had used the right word. There was no other that seemed nearly as appropriate under the circumstances. One week both husbands had been with them; the next they were gone.

"I look into that abyss every night," she added nervously. "It swallows up our bedroom with its darkness. I imagine that Douglas is there somehow, hidden, not able to reach through, but he wants to, he desperately wants to, Heather."

Her words choked in her throat.

"I . . . I still feel him, Heather . . . isn't that something? After two years I still dream of him that way . . . I still sleep on my side of our bed."

Becky's shoulders had been slumping. She straightened them suddenly.

"But we go on with our lives," she said defiantly. "We pick up all the messy little pieces, and put them together, and that's that."

She was fighting the urge to sob.

"I still feel so weak sometimes," Becky went on. "I find myself wanting his hand on my shoulder, his lips next to my ear, that voice of his whispering soothing words. I wait for that, you know. When I feel bad, I think of him and I hesitate. It seems almost that I am waiting for his presence to come out of nowhere and pronounce everything that has happened to be the most vivid nightmare imaginable but that the time has come for it to end."

Becky sighed deeply. "All the books ever written about such matters, all the advice ever offered by well-meaning friends boils down to something so simple, you know—finding the strength to face each day, with the kind of baggage we must carry along with us."

"We've got each other, Becky," Heather told her. "I think

we've known that this might happen and that we've been pre-paring ourselves for it since we met."

Becky smiled with embarrassment.

"My, oh my! Here *you* are consoling me, and yet that's the job *I'm* supposed to have, isn't it?"

"We have no one else, do we?" Heather said, appreciating how her friend felt. "I mean, isn't that truly the case, in the intimate ways that really count? The outside world will do its part in a mechanical and unfeeling way, trying to put a sensitive facade on all this, but it is nothing more than business as usual in any event. There will be any number of letters from the agency, a few phone calls, I'm sure, and then the monthly checks start coming."

She stopped, bitterness gripping her.

"Did you ever wonder about how much of that is conscience money?" she added.

"Have I ever!" Becky answered. "They're saying, 'The job we gave him killed your husband. Here's some cash. Go pay a few bills with it.'"

Typical.

Human beings did work for the agency. After all, their husbands had never ceased *being* human. But for everyone except a handful like Nick Tazelaar and Douglas Huizinga, emotions grew stunted, shapeless, and often just died, replaced by the routine of their work, the need to think furtively—this coup or that covert operation or a thousand other schemes that had to be viewed *without* emotion at the altar of pure pragmatism.

He'd come home after being away for so many weeks, and not be able to look at me straight on. He had done something he was ashamed of, some dirty act that filled him with shame. Sometimes he managed to tell me what it was, sometimes he could do nothing but sink into my arms and cry. . . .

14

Abruptly, Heather walked closer to the edge of the grave, picked up some loose dirt and threw it on top of the dark wood coffin.

"Good-bye, my love," she said softly but with some passion. "I miss you so very much, dearest Nick."

Becky and Heather returned to an awaiting limousine and sobbed together on the way back home.

3

★ ★ ★

During the days that followed, Heather went about the house in a zombielike state, heating up TV dinners when she ate at all, pulling out albums of photos and looking at each one intently, wanting desperately to feel Nick's presence again, if only through memories the shots brought back to her.

She chuckled a few times at some of those memories.

Nick didn't think I could do it, she recalled as she looked at several shots of the two of them inside a helicopter. *But I fooled him. I learned to fly better than he ever imagined I would. I was so happy that he gave me a chance, despite his misgivings, and he was so proud of me that I did something not normally associated with being a "housewife." He called me the greatest, and I told him that I would be nothing without him.*

She slept badly, an hour or two at a time, awakening, tossing, looking at the bright green, neon-like digital numbers on the rectangular clock beside her bed, then closing her eyes again and drifting off until she awakened again, and again, and again—always the same cycle.

At nine o'clock on the seventh morning after Nick's burial, while Heather was still in bed, the phone rang. She groped for the receiver, put it too hard against her ear, hurting herself in the process, then finally croaked a groggy "Hello" into the pearl-white mouthpiece.

"Mrs. Tazelaar," the voice said at the other end. "I really do need to speak with you about something."

"Who is this?" she asked, irritated that the man hadn't seen fit to identify himself right away.

"Oh, sorry. I'm Karl Weatherby. I came to see you, to express the agency's condolences, earlier in the week. I'm sure you remember."

"Yes. I remember. It's early for me, Mr. Weatherby. I haven't been sleeping well. Get to the point, please."

"Excuse me," he said with no hint in his voice that he was embarrassed in the slightest, "but there are some papers that are missing from Nick Tazelaar's files at the office. I was wondering if perhaps he might have taken them home with him before leaving on this, eh, last assignment."

Heather thought for a moment, then informed him that she had no idea if that was the case.

"But I'll be glad to look later today," she replied. "Do call me this evening if you like."

She was about to hang up when Weatherby quickly asked her if she would wait a moment.

"It's fairly important, Mrs. Tazelaar," he insisted. "The papers are, well, top secret. I would like to be there with you when you find them."

Her sleepiness was dissipating. Adrenaline started kicking in, aided by growing irritation over the man's imperious manner.

18

"I will be glad to call you *if* I find anything," she said firmly. "You needn't worry that I will be leafing through the nation's nuclear secrets."

"It's not that, Mrs. Tazelaar."

"Then what *is* it, Mr. Weatherby?"

"The government requires that—"

"Nick worked for the agency, sir. *You* work for the agency. *I,* however, do not. If I am able to find whatever it is that you want, I will call you back. And you can come back here at *my* convenience, period. *That,* sir, is when I will allow you into my house again to pick them up, not before."

She slammed the receiver back on its cradle, anger bringing out perspiration all over her body.

After some toast, coffee, and a small glass of orange juice, Heather called Becky and told her what had happened.

She could hear her friend hesitate for a moment.

"What is it?" she asked.

"Strange," Becky mumbled.

"What's strange?"

"A year ago, just after Douglas disappeared, someone—not this Karl guy, but someone else—called and asked about some papers."

"Did you find any?"

"I did. In a sealed manila envelope. Douglas had written on the front just two letters, or maybe they were initials: MM."

"What was that all about?"

"I don't know. I just handed it over to this drone from the agency who came by a few hours later."

"I wonder if there's any connection?"

"If you find anything, what are you going to do?"

"I can't say. I think, since they were Nick's, I should have

19

some insight into what he was working on when he . . . disappeared."

"They're government property, Heather."

"I realize that. But what could they do to me? Nick gave his life for them. Are they going to send me to prison because I leafed through some homework that he happened to bring home with him?"

"Heather . . . ?" Becky started to ask, tentatively.

"You want to be here, to help me, to see whatever it is yourself, isn't that it?" Heather observed intuitively. "It's all right. Come on over."

"Bless you," Becky added.

"Give me a little while to look human."

"Me, too. It's a sleepy sort of day."

Heather Tazelaar's hand was shaking a bit as she hung up.

Neither of them could find anything special at first, though they looked in every location where Heather thought there might be something that Nick had put away for safekeeping.

"He must be an expert at this sort of thing," Becky suggested. "Unless he left the file someplace else."

"Let's try the attic," Heather said. "There's not much of anything up there, but I can't think of anyplace else now."

The unfinished attic, which Nick and she had intended to make over into a game room "next year," but kept putting off the task, stretched from one end of the house to the other—a large, bare-beamed, uninviting expanse that seemed as dead and incomplete as her life without him surely would prove to be.

It should be filled with the sound of our laughter, she thought, *and now there is nothing, nothing at all except Becky and me pawing over the remains.*

The attic seemed to bear no special fruit for them, and little was found except odds and ends of items that brought back memories for the two of them, since Becky had shared some of the events with the Tazelaars.

A box of color slides.

Heather found it in one corner, among a pile of empty cartons, along with a little battery-powered hand viewer.

"That trip to Europe!" Heather exclaimed as she sat on the floor of the attic. "It was only three years ago."

"Three years," Becky repeated wistfully. "Remember when Douglas and I walked all along the Via Venuto, while you and Nick were quite content to stay behind and explore those ruins at the Forum."

"You two were into looking good," Heather said, her tone soft, her mind filled with those scenes, "while Nick and I favored old things, things that were as ancient as possible. We didn't care what we looked like, just some tattered clothes for climbing around the ruins was OK with us."

Both started laughing.

"How right you are," Becky agreed. "I wanted clothes. You were into history."

"But we both got together at the Mamertine Prison."

"That we did."

It was a time they would never forget, those moments at the miserable place where Paul the apostle had been confined, a cramped and murky little hole in the ground, the dampness certain to rot away anyone's health.

"You started crying as you stood there in the middle of that dreary place," Becky pointed out. "We all thought something might be wrong, that perhaps you had somehow hurt yourself on the way down."

"It hasn't happened since," Heather replied. "I seemed to

be really connected with the Lord then, though I know it's wrong to depend upon *places* or *buildings* or anything else material for that to happen."

"I felt as though two thousand years had evaporated, and Paul was still there, and I was looking at him, weeping over the miserable conditions the Romans had decreed for the greatest of all the apostles."

They sat down on the bare wood floor of the attic.

"Somehow we caught what you were experiencing," Becky recalled. "We caught this sense of great joy but also deep sorrow. Paul was only days away from his so-called execution. He was tired, cold, lonely, and probably sick. Yet he could write such a verse from that spot. We started, together, to repeat it."

I have learned, in whatsoever state I am, therewith to be content. . . .

They hadn't known until later that it was the same location where he put down those words on a scroll of papyrus. And that made the moment, in retrospect, all the more profoundly affecting.

"We had that really bad argument when we returned home," Heather reminded her friend. "I criticized you for being obsessed with clothes and souvenirs and staying only in the plushest hotels. You were deeply offended by what I said and left here, slamming the front door real hard behind you."

Heather wiped some tears from her cheeks.

"I was determined never to speak to you again," Becky admitted. The recollection was a wounding one.

"And I felt the same way, Becky. I thought you were nothing more than a pampered, materialistic phony. But that was before Nick looked at me after I told him what had happened, his expression itself making me feel quite ashamed without, at first, knowing really exactly why."

Heather was holding a photo of her husband that she had snapped in front of the Coliseum. "He was so wise, so kind," she said. "He had such insight into me."

"And everyone else," Becky remarked wistfully. "He and Douglas were perfect friends."

"Nick insisted that I follow him around the house. He pointed to the expensive vases that I had been collecting, the superplush carpeting, the premium wallpaper, the kitchen that just had to have the most technologically advanced appliances or I would never have been satisfied.

"'Are you so different?' he said. 'If what you say is true about Becky, then aren't you just as guilty as you claim she is? But that's not all. Aren't you far *more* hypocritical, getting on her case while ignoring your own dependency? You're as addicted to "things" as an addict is to his drugs.'"

After Heather recalled that encounter, she wanted to stand, surrounded by bare oak studding and fiberglass insulation, and shout, "Forgive me, Nick, my beloved. Please forgive me, dearest!" a thousand times, but instead she just sat there, holding in her emotions as she kept glancing at his photo.

"Let me hold you," Becky said, sensing her friend's state of utter melancholy then.

Heather sobbed as Becky hugged her. A little while later that surge of emotion passed, and they sat on the creaky floor of the attic, talking sporadically, silent just as often.

"Every wife who loves her husband feels the way we do when they die," Heather said. "But most of those *other* wives, well, they get to give their men that one last kiss or tenderly touch his cheek. You and I . . . we had the husbands we loved ruthlessly ripped out of our lives without warning. We had no preparation. It's unfair, this whole business is so unfair."

"And no children," Becky added. "We have that bond, too.

We are alone in homes that were supposed to house large families, and now we must return to their emptiness."

Becky shook her head.

"What?" Heather asked.

"The warnings," she replied. "We did have some, you know, from the beginning, in fact."

"I don't understand."

"We knew something *could* happen because of the work they did. Let's use the right word this time, Heather. They weren't agents. Nor undercover couriers. Plain and simple, they were *spies!* When all the polite-sounding titles or terms are cut away, that really is what's underneath. There's no predictability for spies, Heather. They can be alive one day, murdered the next. I'm surprised that more aren't Christians. How could they face such danger without the sure knowledge of what death holds for them?"

She leaned forward, looking at Heather straight on.

"None of us has any excuses. We've lived with the possibility of disaster day in and day out for a very long time. How many times, when Nick was away, did you hesitate before answering the phone?

"For me, with Douglas, it was a dozen times a day, maybe more. Or the doorbell . . . and I'd answer it, and whenever I saw a stranger standing just outside, my heart would nearly freeze, Heather. Was *he* the one to bring me the agency's 'sincere condolences'? Yet it was always a salesman of some kind or somebody from the electric company—you know, that kind of stranger.

"I faced the same routine again and again until, one day, it wasn't the same at all, and what I had feared all along, what I had *anticipated,* was true. There was this stranger, and he gave me those condolences, and I wanted to die, I wanted to die right then, and not have to turn around and face that empty house."

She smiled sympathetically.

"It hasn't been long in your case," she said. "The pain is bad for you right now—believe me, I *know* how bad—but it *does* pass. Yes, you have this ghastly hole in your life, and that doesn't go away, but somehow you survive, not the same, of course, and there will be, for a long while, bouts with despair that pop up without warning, but please believe that you *do* get through it all."

She licked her lips.

"I'm dry," she said. "How about you?"

"Me, too," Heather agreed. "I'll go downstairs and—"

"You just sit there and relax. I'm waiting on *you* for a change."

As Becky stood, she added, "I'll go ahead and make some fresh iced tea for the two of us, OK?"

"Fine," Heather replied, then remembered something she had meant to point out before. "Hey, I forgot to tell you on the way up, but watch out for two loose boards near the top of the stairs. Luckily, we missed stepping on them earlier, but you should be a bit careful now. They're just to the left of—"

Becky screamed. She had walked to the stairs at the other end of the attic. She had been thrown off balance and had fallen against a stud in the attic but was not hurt. The floorboard had broken in half when she put her weight on it. If she had not acted quickly, a jagged end could have jammed deeply into her leg. But she pulled it up in a split second, only grazing one side just a bit without actually breaking the skin.

"If only I had told you before this," Heather said, shaking nearly as much as her friend, as they both leaned against the wall.

25

"It happens, it happens," Becky told her, slightly out of breath. "No injuries, other than my nerves."

Heather smiled. "You're a tough soul."

"Only on the outside. What you see isn't what you get. I'm a bundle of paranoid hang-ups inside."

"I don't believe it."

"Good! I was just kidding."

Heather bent down, toward the broken wood.

"I wonder why Nick didn't have this fixed. It wasn't normal for him to let anything dangerous like this go by without taking care of it."

"Maybe he just forgot. After all, how much time did Nick spend up here alone in the attic while he had a wife like you waiting downstairs?"

"A lot," Heather said matter-of-factly. "He was up here a—"

She and Becky glanced quickly at one another.

"You're thinking the same thing I am, aren't you?" she remarked.

Becky nodded.

Heather bent down and carefully pulled back the fragmented section of wood that had caused the accident.

Underneath was a manila envelope.

On the front were just two letters: *MM*.

4
★ ★ ★

Hours later, they both had read much of the contents, some pages typed, some handwritten, the rest preserved on 35-mm slides that they looked at through the hand-held, battery-operated viewer.

Becky cried as the two of them sat on the curved, dark blue sectional sofa in the living room, the contents of that envelope spread out on an inlaid-marble coffee table in front of them.

"Douglas had to have had the same file," she said. "Douglas must have been part of this, this—"

She could not finish the sentence.

"Then why did it take so long for my Nick to be . . . to be disposed of?" Heather asked with great difficulty. "More than a year has passed since Douglas disappeared. I don't understand why there was this kind of a delay."

After sniffing back her tears, Becky considered what Heather had said.

"Because . . . because it would look strange," she said slowly. "I mean, two agents gone at the same time. They *had* to wait. Don't you see that?"

Heather nodded.

"You're right," she replied. "Any connection could not be made so easily between the two."

Her eyes widened.

"But it's not just Nick and Douglas! The report claimed that there were three agents involved in this. Two are gone. The third may still be alive!"

"And when will *he* be *terminated?*"

Heather leaned back against the welcome softness of the massive sofa, dozens of sheets of paper scattered on her lap along with newspaper clippings—whatever was not on the coffee table. She idly picked up one of the latter and glanced yet again at the headline: ACTRESS COMMITS SUICIDE.

"All these years," Heather mumbled.

"Frankly I didn't like that woman's morals at all," Becky admitted, "but to be murdered by—!"

She cleared her throat, at the same time trying to steady her nerves.

"She trusted the president of the United States and the attorney general. She trusted those two until the end."

The reports on Heather's lap detailed how misplaced that trust had been. After seducing an actress whose emotional stability had been tenuous for many years, the now-deceased Kennedy brothers abruptly lost interest and went on to yet other extramarital liaisons, in and out of the White House.

"They never considered women to be anything but sources of pleasure for them," Heather remarked. "And yet so many people consider JFK to be some kind of idol on a pedestal, his memory to be cherished."

"Where was the love in any of their relationships?" Becky went on. "Where was anything but their own selfish interests?"

Heather had clenched her hands into fists and was shaking

28

them in front of her, trying to deal with the most scalding anger she had ever felt.

I know feeling like this is wrong, Lord, she admitted to herself. *But then how can I react any other way?* Finally she stood and paced the tongue-and-groove floor.

"I can't believe that Douglas never told me anything," she mused. "I can't believe I detected no clues whatever. How could I have been as stupid as that?"

"I didn't either," Heather replied. "Our men kept their lives as compartmentalized as possible. That was why we stayed as happy as we were. They thought literally that what we didn't know couldn't hurt us. They never allowed their work into the house, taking it into their family lives with them."

"And yet they did, Heather," Becky protested. "They failed because they couldn't cut off the awful things in their professional lives simply by leaving some folders at the office and then coming home. It wasn't that easy. What they did affected what they were. I saw the deterioration in Douglas over a period of time. I saw his moods darken. Toward the end, he jumped almost anytime the phone rang."

Her insides trembled as images returned, one after the other, images of a man once happy, once giving of himself, gradually turning inside himself, blocking her out more and more often.

"I tried so hard to break past that wall that was going up brick by brick," Becky said. "I begged him to let me help, to let me have a chance to help him deal with whatever was eating at him."

She turned and, still standing, looked down at Heather.

"But he wouldn't. Just a few days before he died, he gave me one little clue, just a hint of why he was so determined to keep me at a distance. You know what he said?"

Heather shook her head.

"Douglas said to me, 'I can *never* tell you. It's important, beloved, that you know *nothing*. If you're ever questioned, if they ever pressure you, you can be honest, you can tell them the truth. Their kind are masters at lying. They know when others are lying. I *have* to see that you're safe. I have to *know* that you won't be harmed.'"

For several minutes she just stood there, saying nothing further, trying to get her emotions back under control. Then she sat down again, took several of the sheets of paper from Heather's lap, and leafed through them one more time.

"Marilyn is killed, then that gangster takes out a contract on the Kennedys. And somehow, the CIA and some arms dealers are involved."

. . . some arms dealers are involved.

They looked at one another. Both were feeling cold then, cold throughout every muscle, every nerve in their body.

"They know that you have this," Becky commented.

"They don't," Heather replied. "Nick could have hidden it anywhere else. In a safe-deposit box. In another country altogether."

"Then why did that character come here, why did he grill you about the file?"

"He was probing. When he woke me up so early in the morning, Becky, I was *very* convincing when I told him that I would call when I found it."

"I don't think it's that simple, Heather. As our husbands found out over the years, lying is an expert business. It's almost an art form. They just might think you're lying to buy yourself time."

"Time? For what? I don't understand."

"For exposing the whole rats' nest."

Heather gulped a couple of times.

CIA bigwigs controlled by the arms industry with huge amounts of bribe money flowing into carefully disguised bank accounts all over the world. For the arms merchants, though, such sums probably came out of their petty cash reserves. The real stakes were into the billions of dollars.

"Is it likely that the whole agency *hasn't* been corrupted?" she ventured. "That we could get some help from those not involved in this conspiracy?"

"That's possible. I don't see how the entire CIA could have been drawn into this. Robert Gates may not be the world's warmest, most lovable personality, but he seems thoroughly incorruptible, Heather."

Becky's eyes darted nervously from side to side almost as an involuntary reaction to the thoughts that were surfacing.

"No, I suspect it's just a few of them, an influential few. If clandestine operations can be hidden from the president of the United States—which was what was said about Irangate—then keeping even someone like Robert Gates, not to mention other lesser figures, in the dark should be a piece of cake."

"I've got to study all of this more and pray for some guidance," Heather said wearily. "I don't know what to think, what to do."

Becky tried to smile reassuringly but failed.

"Well . . . I have to go now," she said with false nonchalance. "I need to do some shopping, stuff like that."

Becky left, and Heather remained on the sofa, dreading an even closer look at the file contents.

Oh Lord, she prayed silently, *without the knowledge that Nick is walking the streets of your glorious heaven, angels by his side, I wouldn't want to go on. There would be nothing left, no hope at all.*

Then she stood, looking at the living room, remembering how she and Nick had picked out everything together—the furniture, the rug, the drapes, even the paint for the walls, with earth tones dominating.

She thought of lonely, wonderful Becky.

"Now I have only you," she whispered as she closed her eyes and tried to deal with the anguish that had returned full force.

5
★ ★ ★

Five minutes past midnight.

Heather had had the various sheets strewn across her bed. She was tired after going through them again. As she finally relaxed, half-asleep, she thought over some portions of what the contents had revealed.

Operation Paperclip.

That had been the start of it, according to the file. That had been what caught Nick's interest, along with the other two agents.

Heather had started to piece together the puzzle. It happened because of a single phone call, beginning the earliest stages of Nick's involvement. . . .

"Operation Paperclip," the man's voice over the receiver had told Nick.

"I beg your pardon," he had said. "What did you say about—?"

"Operation Paperclip went crazy," the voice continued in a monotone. "It embedded into the mainstream of American government and the military too many of the *wrong* kinds of people. They're quite *evil.*"

"I have no idea what you're talking about," Nick said. "What in the world is Operation Paperclip?"

"Look up the file. There must be a file. It won't give you all the facts. But it will be a start."

Click.

Nick held the receiver dumbly in his hand for a few seconds, then disconnected. An instant later, he dialed the agency switchboard.

"This is Tazelaar," he said. "Did you just put through a call for me?"

"Yes sir, I did," the cigarette-husky voice replied.

"Was it over the transom? Or did they ask specifically for me?"

"The call was directly for you, sir."

Nick leaned back in his chair, realizing that tens of thousands of crackpot calls came in annually. But these were usually directed at anyone who happened to be available.

He knows my name, Nick thought. *He called with something very specific in mind, and it was directed at me.*

He had told the caller that Operation Paperclip rang no bells, and he meant it, but as he repeated those words, bits and pieces of recollection floated to the surface of his mind.

Paperclip . . . Paperclip . . . after World War II . . . it had something to do with Nazi scientists and others from the Third Reich.

He faced the computer screen on his desk and typed out a file access code, adding PAPERCLIP.

DENIED. TOP SECURITY CLEARANCE ONLY.

"What in the—?" he started to say out loud.

He tried again, this time adding to the code the special priority clearance number that he had been assigned.

What scrolled across the screen was a routine collection of information about a post–World War II project that gleaned from Germany the top physicists, biologists, and other scientists from Hitler's elite group.

"Instead of working for the devil, they used their skills for the United States," Nick mumbled out loud. "What's the big deal?"

He was about to refile what he had read, turn off the computer, and go home, when the phone rang. Since it was after hours, whoever was calling had access to his direct number.

"This is Douglas," the voice said. "I got the strangest call."

"Anything to do with Operation Paperclip?"

"Exactly. You, too?"

"Just a little while ago. I booted up the file. Nothing special in it, as far as I can see."

"Crank call, then?"

"Maybe. . . ."

"You don't sound convinced, old boy."

"It was the way this guy spoke."

"Like he was on a mission of some sort?"

"Like he really meant every word. Like he was sitting on something so stinking important that he was willing to risk a great deal."

"What do we do?"

"Dismiss it from our minds. If the guy calls again, well, that's another story, I suppose."

"See you later, buddy. Give Heather my best."

"And tell Rebecca I love her. She's just great, in my book."

Nick hung up, smiling. He and Douglas Huizinga had been

friends for years. The two of them had worked together on a number of intriguing cases. Their wives were close as well.

He had slipped on his coat and was standing when the phone rang again.

"What did you forget to tell me—?" he started to ask.

The voice that interrupted him wasn't Douglas's.

The caller had asked them to meet him in a well-liked cellar restaurant located within a block of Embassy Row. Nick and Douglas were familiar with the place, having eaten there a number of times.

The two men arrived separately, driving their own cars to the spot. Nick got there first, followed by Douglas less than five minutes later.

They stood outside, reading the name on the red awning over the restaurant's entrance.

"Memories," Douglas said, sighing. "We really pigged out here the first time, remember?"

"Man, you bet I do," Nick replied. "I know you and I are oinkers, but the women, hey, they almost out-ate us."

They went inside and gave their coats to the attendant. The voice over the phone had told them exactly where to sit. So they headed toward that booth, their eyes smarting from the cocktail crowd's heavy layer of smoke.

A short, thin, baggy-eyed man in rumpled clothes was waiting for them.

They introduced themselves.

"And *your* name, sir?" Nick asked.

"Sidney Rosenblatt," he said, gesturing for them to sit down.

Almost immediately they noticed the numbers tattooed on his wrist.

"Which camp, Mr. Rosenblatt?" Douglas asked.

"It was Mauthausen. I compliment your alertness," the man replied. "I suggest you turn that gift to our surroundings and be on guard against anyone who appears to be eavesdropping on us."

"Too noisy," Douglas pointed out.

"You're right."

"Was that a test?" Douglas asked.

"And a very poor one. Forgive me, please."

"Tell us what is going on," Nick remarked not sympathetically. "That would be apology enough."

"You have read about Operation Paperclip?"

Both men nodded.

"What is in that 'official' file is, I am sure, only the public-relations side of the picture."

"It was classified as restricted," Nick pointed out. "Only those with top-priority clearance can gain access to the file. That's hardly necessary for anything that is PR puffery only."

"Or an attempt to make the false seem real."

Nick and Douglas glanced at one another. Their palms were beginning to sweat, a career-long indication that they had stepped into something that would take them far away from the routine.

Rosenblatt ordered a vodka martini.

"Will you be my guest?" he asked.

"We don't drink," Nick told him.

"Health or religious reasons?"

"A little of both."

"How can you not drink and yet do what you must do in order to become such respected operatives?"

"How do you know we're so respected?" Nick asked.

"Any information on anyone is available for a price."

"Go ahead, Mr. Rosenblatt."

"An element has been successful at infiltrating the governmental, military, judicial, and business communities in this country that can be traced directly to the first participants in Operation Paperclip."

"Surely you're not trying to get us to listen to yet another hare-brained conspiracy theory," Douglas protested angrily.

The man took a glossy photo out of his pocket and put it on top of the table in front of them.

They recognized it immediately.

A postmortem shot of the body of John Fitzgerald Kennedy.

"And next you're going to blame Lyndon Baines Johnson, the Warren Commission, and who knows what others you can throw together!" Nick said, starting to stand as he did so. "Not interested, Mr. Rosenblatt."

Rosenblatt sat there, chuckling a bit, as he said, "That was my reaction when I first stumbled into this cesspool. I thought my old anti-German, antimilitary phobias had kicked in again. When you once have been the object of all of that venom, when you are that piece of flesh the Nazis are trying to ground into so much pulp, getting into such a mind-set, trust me, is instinctive after awhile."

Nick hesitated, then decided to give the man a little more time. Douglas followed suit.

"Go on," Nick said, sitting back down.

"You mentioned Lyndon Baines Johnson," Rosenblatt continued. "The story that Kennedy was preparing to get out of Vietnam happens to be true. So, what happens? JFK is assassinated and LBJ begins immediately to expand U.S. involvement in Vietnam. Where there is war, there are huge arms sales!"

"No sir, it has *never* been proven true or false," Douglas

interjected. "I happen to believe that it is little more than a media-concocted myth."

Rosenblatt reached into his pocket and produced a sheet of paper that he put on top of the photograph.

"Read that," he said simply.

A confidential memo to Robert McNamara, then secretary of defense.

After reading the contents, Nick audibly let out his breath, and Douglas fell back into his seat.

"It could be a forgery," Nick suggested.

"Anything could be anything if you want to believe that it's nothing," Rosenblatt replied. "For the moment, let's assume that it is genuine. And let's assume that certain people found out."

"So the military-industrial complex was behind the assassination?" Nick offered. "That seems to be where you're heading. Mr. Rosenblatt, this isn't news. It's not even decent supposition anymore. Oliver Stone said as much in his film *JFK*. If I am little inclined to believe *him*, since everything he directs betrays a little of his own hidden agenda, why should I give your so-called information, or you, for that matter, any credence?"

"Because not even Mr. Stone dared to hint at who was *behind* them!" Rosenblatt exclaimed, jabbing a finger in the air in front of them.

"Behind the military-industrial complex?" Douglas mused out loud. "You're saying that they're not the devil himself?"

"That *is* what I'm saying, my friend. They are but the puppets or, shall we say, the arms addicts. To go after *them* can be likened to throwing a few low-life drug pushers in jail and then proclaiming to one and all that the war on drugs is being won. It will *never* be won until the men *feeding* the system are captured. *They are the truly evil ones!*"

Nick noticed that the palms of both hands had continued to sweat. He glanced at Douglas, who nodded, indicating the same was true for him.

"Wickedness in high places," Nick mumbled.

"You quote from the Bible," Rosenblatt remarked. "Let me go farther than just what that particular verse suggests. There are, in this world, men so corrupt, men so enslaved to despicable acts, acts that become the lifeblood of their very existence, that they are not unwilling to sacrifice entire countries if any genocide on that scale can turn them a profit."

"And this has something to do with Operation Paperclip?" Nick asked. "What is the connection?"

"Paperclip was the mechanism, the structure," Rosenblatt told them. "It allowed scores of ruthless and sadistic men to escape punishment simply because the United States government or, I should say, the U.S. military establishment, wanted the *knowledge* they possessed: knowledge about weapons, knowledge about nerve gas and rockets, and a great deal more."

"While the Nuremburg trials were going on, meting out punishment to Göring and others," Douglas said, "other Nazis struck a gold mine and sidestepped any prosecution whatsoever?"

"The Paperclip file says that the scientists and others were completely exonerated," Nick put in.

"What would you expect?" Rosenblatt asserted. "The attempted Watergate and Irangate cover-ups were child's play, my friends, partly because the masterminds were aging professionals whose skill had gone downhill or, in a couple of instances, bright but inexperienced newcomers to deception—

and, after all, they ultimately failed. So far, Paperclip hasn't. It's been a roaring success! And Wernher von Braun is a classic example of this success."

"He's considered a genuine hero, even now," Nick protested. "He supposedly beat the Nazi system and joined *us*. How can you offer this man as a classic example of anything but redemption?"

"Or as a demon posing as an angel of light perhaps?" Rosenblatt replied, giving them another biblical reference.

He cleared his throat, then continued: "As a Jew, I pay not so much attention to Christian theology. But that is one portion of the New Testament that seems totally to have all of this in profound focus."

He pulled out a manila envelope.

"Take this with you," he said as he glanced at his watch. "I must go now. We meet again in a few days."

Abruptly, Sidney Rosenblatt stood and started to walk off without shaking hands or saying good-bye, but then turned and smiled as he remarked, "Mr. Tazelaar, I suppose you've heard this before but, truly, it *is* amazing how much you look like John Kennedy!"

6

Oh, Nick, you did, you did. I used to tease you about it, especially after all those assassination theories started to surface. . . .

Heather had a pounding headache as she put the file aside for a moment and closed her eyes.

Nick, what destructive forces were arrayed against you, my love? she thought, as images of a so-handsome and dashing Wernher von Braun, smiling beneficently, flashed into her mind.

As she fought to subdue another burst of rage, one of many over the past week, Heather went on reading, startled anew by the facts regarding this so-called hero who had done so much to help the U.S. effort in space.

According to the file, Operation Paperclip was unofficially constructed around the man. He was the star player, the prime "catch," whisked from continued Nazi associations during the postwar era when a host of the unrepentant surviving members of Hitler's "team" went underground, some of them ferreted out over the coming decades but some not, despite the best efforts of Simon Wiesenthal and others, surviving to perpetrate *in absentia* the debased and inhuman dreams of their *fuehrer*.

Wernher von Braun was supposed to be an example of a rehabilitated Nazi, someone who had shed the old barbarism and become civilized once again, yet he had been caught trying to smuggle secret documents to various operatives in Germany *soon after he joined Operation Paperclip!*

During the war, he also had been part of numerous slave-labor meetings involving plans that would bring more French prisoner participation in underground laboratories, where experiments ranged from forcing the helpless to drink seawater, to finding out the effects of oxygen deprivation. A large majority of those subjected to the suffering that resulted died in the midst of the most wrenching pain!

"'And yet von Braun is exonerated from all of this, including other questionable postwar behavior,'" Heather read out loud, "'because he had become involved with the U.S. military. Fellow war criminals were hanged after the Nuremberg trials, *but not such a great scientist!'"*

She shuddered with disgust, as she knew Nick must have done at the time he had read what she now was reading, but she soon realized that it all got worse, that von Braun was not simply a rotten apple that threatened to spoil the entire operation. There may have been nothing *but* men of his type, guilty of similar or worse crimes, men who constituted the *entire* gallery of Paperclip insiders.

Including the first appointed director of the Kennedy Space Center at Cape Canaveral.

Kurt Debus.

Debus had been absolved through Operation Paperclip of a range of war crimes, neatly avoiding virtually certain prosecution. Investigation showed that he had proudly served as a devout member of the Nazi SS, the SA, and two other groups formed by Hitler. Three years before World War II ended, he had betrayed a colleague, who was then grabbed by the Gestapo, tortured, and held for so-called trial.

More evidence of Debus's wholehearted support of and participation in the Nazi cause was turned up and presented to the officials in charge of Operation Paperclip at the time, but all of it was dismissed on the specious grounds that "his value to us as a nation does sufficiently outweigh any crimes against humanity that Kurt Debus may have committed," according to the Deputy Director of Paperclip, who added that Debus was "simply doing what was considered patriotic at the time."

Heather felt the blood drain from her face.

The military sold its soul to the devil in order to be able to gain access to some of the devil's devices!

But she saw, from other portions of the file, that the corruption went beyond the military and, for that matter, the scientific community. It had worked its way into the very fabric of government itself, with members of the cabinets of various presidents implicated as well as those elected to Congress.

Heather turned one particular page almost with dread. There she read what had been uncovered about Lyndon Baines Johnson: allegations that he had been involved in some way in the assassination of JFK or, at least, had known about it and had done nothing to stop what had been set in motion.

"For years, while in the Senate, long before he became vice president, Johnson had been maintaining the most intimate personal relationships with certain key defense firm CEOs and others," Nick had written on a yellow ruled sheet of paper. "Arms dealers were another group. Lyndon used their rifles, their ammunition, partied with them, did innumerable favors

for them, which were channeled through respectable front or-
ganizations such as the American Firearms Congress."

*Oh, Nick, how could you have lived with this, kept it to your-
self, without ever giving me some kind of hint so that I could
offer you some support?* Heather thought with an edge of real
anger.

And yet, suddenly she recalled there had been clues of a
sort—whether Nick meant to betray these or not—night after
night when he hardly spoke, his attention fixed only on some
documentary about the Vietnam War, entranced by scenes of
the battlefield, together with atrocities committed by both
sides, and he would turn away and there would be tears in his
eyes. She assumed that this was "merely" an emotional reaction to the carnage and the tragedy it represented.

Tragedy was the right word, Heather reasoned, as though
able to "connect" with Nick himself. *But it was a tragedy beyond anything the newsreel cameras and commentators alone
captured.*

All because greedy and nameless men saw an opportunity
to make the kinds of huge profits that were invariably part of
the process of unleashing a giant war machine. Families lost
husbands and sons and were plunged into enormous debt as
part of the process of trying to keep together in the wake of
such severe loss, yet these monstrous individuals lost nothing
but their consciences as billions of dollars poured into their
pockets from all over the world.

"The Lord never said it would be easy to get up each morning and face life," Nick had written on another sheet. "What I
have learned, now, makes me wonder how I am indeed able to
endure such knowledge as this without resorting to the taking
of my own life with the quick cut of a knife or a pistol to my
head or perhaps a handful of quite innocent-looking pills.

Praise God in heaven that I have someone like Heather with me. Even though she is ignorant of what has happened as a result of Operation Paperclip, she gives me much-needed strength simply by loving me."

She clutched that sheet of paper and held it to her chest, and in that instant, all the grief she had experienced earlier seemed as nothing compared to what then took over her mind and heart.

Heather had fallen asleep with the file still spread out over her bed. When she awoke, the clock on the nightstand next to her read three o'clock. She was still holding that last note written by Nick.

. . . *simply by loving me.*

Her eyes focused again on those words.

"How could it be otherwise?" she asked out loud. "How could I feel anything but love for you, Nick?"

She sighed, then saw the randomly strewn sheets and decided to gather them together and put them back in the manila folder. As she held the last piece in her hand, a newspaper clipping, she caught her breath.

A sound.

Not a normal nighttime sound, like an owl perhaps or some cat fight or a dog barking. No, not that kind of sound.

Someone walking. A board in the stairs leading up to the second floor. Someone walking up those stairs.

She hesitated a moment, then climbed slowly out of bed, heading toward the dresser bureau on the opposite side of the bedroom, intending to get a revolver that Nick had kept there, just in case.

Too late.

A tall, broad-shouldered figure in a ski mask crashed open

the bedroom door. As soon as he saw that she was aware of him, he lunged for her, knocking her off her feet and onto the thickly carpeted floor. He smelled of cigarettes and liquor, and she gagged because the odor was so intense.

His hands folded around her throat.

She jammed her right knee upward and hit him in the crotch. He fell off her, groaning, but against the bureau, preventing her from opening a drawer and getting the pistol.

She headed for the open doorway and made it to the stairs before the intruder was on her again. They both tumbled down the stairs and hit the floor at the bottom with jarring abruptness.

Heather became dizzy, at first not even able to get to her feet without simply falling again. She turned her head, saw the man lying still, apparently unconscious.

I am strong enough, she told herself. *I am going to get up, to stand, and do what it takes to call for help or defend myself!*

She got weakly to her feet, concentrating on rushing out to the kitchen, toward a drawer with some very large knives in it. Once she had a firm grip on the handle of one of these, she was going to call the police and tell them—

Heather never made it that far. She had reached the drawer and had pulled out a knife with a ten-inch blade when she felt something hit her hard against the back of her head.

She fell, the knife dropping from her hand, and she saw the intruder kick it to one side as he reached down, pulled her up by her hair, and snapped her head back.

She had no strength left. The kitchen was spinning. She could smell those disgusting odors coming from him. She was ready to die. She felt almost relieved because dying meant that she no longer would be without Nick.

Suddenly the man released her. Heather managed to grab

hold of the back of a black, wrought-iron kitchen chair and steady herself.

He pulled the mask off his head in a frenzied motion, and Heather saw his face contorted with pain. He staggered a couple of steps, then tumbled forward, a little cry escaping his lips as he hit the floor.

Heather could see a long-bladed knife protruding from his back, blood seeping from around the edges.

Becky Huizinga stood next to him, looking first at her now-empty left hand, then at the body directly in front of her, then at Heather, before her own face abruptly grew quite pale. She fainted, falling beside the man she had just stabbed to death.

7

★ ★ ★

"What do we do? There's a corpse in the kitchen!" Becky exclaimed after she had regained consciousness and Heather had helped her to a comfortable chair in the living room. "I stuck a knife in his back! Did you hear that little groan? He died then—oh Heather, he died right before our eyes."

Heather was sitting on the padded arm of a floral-patterned easy chair, holding her friend's ample hand, her own insides shaking along with Becky's, neither of them wanting ever again to go back into the kitchen, to see that body again, nor the puddle of blood on the floor.

"He was trying to kill me," Heather said. "You saved my life. It could have been me lying there instead of him. What made you come over just then?"

"I heard noise," Becky replied. "You screamed, you know."

"I didn't realize that."

"Oh, did you scream! I heard other noises seconds later. Before that, I couldn't sleep, so I got up and went out on the front porch. I was standing there, getting some fresh air, thinking what it would

51

be like if, suddenly, Douglas got out of a car and walked up to me and we hugged, and I had him back at last. Your hollering snapped me out of that nonsense. So I ran back inside, grabbed whatever I could that seemed like a good weapon, and hurried over."

She turned toward the kitchen.

"What do we do, Heather?"

"I don't know. I don't know who to call. Nick never introduced me to anyone at the agency. Douglas was the mutual friend we had. I don't know—"

That realization sank in for both of them, because it reminded them how completely their lives had been intertwined with their husbands'. It was one thing to learn how to get used to not having their men around them any more. That was hard enough, tearing up their insides and leaving in its wake countless nights when there would be little sleep. But, now, in just the sort of situation when their husbands would know exactly what to do, neither of them could be certain at all what their next step should be.

"I feel so stupid, so helpless!" Heather exclaimed. "How I depended upon Nick, how much I ended up needing him."

"And neither of us made any preparation for the possibility that, someday, they might not be around, that we would survive them and have to go on with our lives," Becky added. "How could we have been so foolish? There was danger all the time in their professions. Tragedy was always a potential threat, Heather. Yet we just clung to the fantasy that nothing would change, that they would be safe no matter what happened!"

There could be no more fantasies, no more crutches in their lives. The loss of their husbands had started that awareness in a stark manner, and now the dead body in a pool of blood just a few yards away had confirmed it.

"If we *knew* someone who could help," Heather said in frustration. "I mean, how can we call the police? What would we say?"

Becky turned, looked up at her.

"We tell them the truth," she said.

"About the file, about—?"

"We tell them that there was an intruder, and only that. If you get right down to it, we can't be certain that there is any connection. It may be nothing more than a coincidence."

Heather paused, thinking over her friend's words, then remarked, "You're right. The police will take the body away and call it all self-defense. And that will be the end of it all."

"Stop it, Heather. You know that may not be what happens. If that man came here for the file, whoever sent him is going to try again. The only reason the same thing didn't happen with me is that a drone from the agency got to me first."

"Karl-somebody tried," Heather acknowledged. "If I had known, if I could have handed the file to him, then—" She jumped to her feet. "Listen to what we're both saying!" she said almost in a shout.

"What do you mean?" Becky asked. "You've lost me."

"You said that the only reason you didn't have somebody sneak into your house in the middle of the night is that the agency got to you first."

Becky's eyes widened. "And *you* started to say that if you had found the file, and been able to give it to Karl-somebody, then none of *this* would have happened."

Heather felt dizzy. She stumbled back onto the sofa opposite the chair in which Becky was sitting.

"It's ridiculous," she said, "just craziness on our part. We're saying the agency has some connection with this, that this guy was part of their operation, and was sent to . . . to—"

"We search his pockets," Becky reasoned. "We look for whatever identification we can."

"Would he carry anything as incriminating as a CIA employee's card?" Heather posed skeptically.

"In the United States there hasn't been so much secrecy. You know as well as I do that they usually work under cover only on a foreign assignment. Besides, they can't officially go about their business here on home turf. It's forbidden by law, at least as an independent act."

"But they can work in concert with the FBI," Heather continued. The Feds in effect hire them as consultants, especially if terrorists or whatever may be involved."

Both stood and walked slowly toward the kitchen, half hoping that somehow the man wasn't dead after all, that he had managed to get up on his own power and slip out the back door.

He was still there. Lying face down. His arms and legs spread out at awkward angles.

Heather and Becky glanced at him, then at one another, their eyes asking the question, *Who goes first?*

Heather bent down, tried the trouser pockets first. She could get to these without moving the body.

Nothing.

"His wallet's probably in his jacket, I mean, it's less likely to drop out from there," Becky suggested.

But he was on his chest. That meant turning him over!

Becky bent down next to Heather, and they started to roll the body over on its back. The knife, slightly dislodged from the man's fall, now slipped out onto the floor. Heather couldn't bear to touch it, and simply rolled the body over, hiding the weapon from view. The left hand, which had been resting in a puddle of blood, slapped across Becky's face.

She dropped the body and screamed as she fell backward against the refrigerator.

"His blood!" she cried. "It's on my cheek, it's . . . it's on . . ."

Heather rushed over to her and shook her large frame.

"I'll wipe it off," she said as calmly as she could manage, though her own insides were threatening to rebel. "I'll get a towel and moisten it with some water, and that will take care of the problem."

After she had grabbed a towel from a rack next to the sink and turned on the faucet, holding the towel under it for a couple of seconds, she hurried back to her friend, who was standing up straight now but still trembling.

"Down the drain!" Becky said sheepishly after her face and neck had been cleaned. "There goes my grand old image of strength and stability in the midst of any crisis."

"Neither of us is strong enough *alone,*" Heather reminded her.

They went back to the body and managed to turn it over. Heather unzipped the brown leather jacket and searched inside for a pocket that might contain the man's wallet.

He's cold already, and yet his eyes are open. Oh Lord, help me not to look at them anymore, she thought, hoping that she wouldn't suddenly break down as Becky had done.

She found it.

The wallet was burgundy eel skin, seemed nearly brand-new, and was thick with credit cards, a driver's license, several hundred dollars in cash, but no CIA identification card.

"It's not here," Heather said. "We were wrong."

"Thinking that he's involved with the agency? Or that he'd be carrying something so obvious with him?"

"I guess you're right. So we don't know anything more now."

"We don't. Let's call the police and get it over with."

There was a phone on the kitchen wall, next to the refrigerator. As Heather was reaching for it, the lights in the house abruptly went out, and they were surrounded by darkness.

"How stupid!" Becky exclaimed. "We should have known."

"Known what?" Heather asked.

"This guy's partner—we didn't think about his partner."

"Like Nick without—"

"Douglas!"

"Upstairs," Heather said, her voice dropping to a whisper. "Nick kept a gun hidden upstairs. We've got to—"

She didn't get a chance to finish her sentence. Someone came crashing through the back door. He was even bigger than the first man—taller, broader. He caught one glimpse of the body on the floor, then threw his head back and yelled in rage. He lunged for Becky. Before he could touch her, she had doubled up her right hand into a fist and clobbered him across the jaw. He yelled in pain but didn't stop and landed a punch of his own in her midsection. As she was falling, she managed to grab him around the neck and hold on, pulling him down with her by her sheer weight.

"Upstairs!" Becky yelled. "Get the gun!"

"No!" Heather told her friend as she searched wildly for something else to use as a weapon, because she knew that by the time she was able to get to the gun and was back downstairs again, Becky might be dead.

A metal pan was hanging from a rack on the wall behind the sink.

She grabbed the handle and whacked the man across the

back of his head with it. He fell to one side as Becky released her hold on his neck.

Heather rushed to Becky and bent down beside her.

"How bad are you?" she asked.

"Blubber helps little in life except at moments like this," Becky replied good-naturedly. "There's hardly any pain. I—"

Her eyes widened.

Behind them, the second man was on his feet already. This time he reached into a holster near his armpit and pulled out a pistol.

"You killed my friend!" he yelled.

He aimed the gun at Becky and pulled the trigger.

The shot caught her in the shoulder and flung her large form back against some kitchen cabinets.

Before he could fire again, Heather leapt upward from her half-sitting position and flung herself against the man. But she was much lighter than Becky, and he only staggered a bit without going down.

He turned the gun on her, a smile crossing his rough-hewn face.

A shot rang out.

His body crumpled to the floor, only a few inches from his partner's.

Heather and Becky glanced toward the back doorway.

Karl-somebody stood there, leaning against the frame! Both hands were folded around a pistol of his own. He replaced it in his holster, then used a tiny mobile phone to dial a number and bark a cryptic demand into it. There was an argument, but apparently he won it, and then he disconnected.

"I'm the third agent mentioned in the file," he said hurriedly. "You have nothing to fear from me. In fifteen minutes, a car will pick us up and take us directly to a site where a heli-

Roger Elwood

copter will be waiting. But now we'll detour, temporarily, to a doctor whose office is adjacent to his home. He'll hate being awakened at this hour, but he *is* trustworthy—and he can treat Mrs. Huizinga better than I'll do in just a moment with any first-aid materials you have here."

He paused, calming his own shaky nerves.

"Then we have to leave," he added. "The helicopter . . . we *have* to get on it!"

8
★ ★ ★

While they waited, Karl Weatherby explained why he happened to be at the house.

"To be honest, I was going to do exactly what *they* apparently had hoped to do," he admitted.

"Break in and find the file?" Heather asked incredulously. "In that case, what's the difference between you and them?"

"A big one—you see, I knew where the file was. I thought I could retrieve it and get out without anyone perceiving that I was ever here. Besides, I already know what's in the file. Truthfully, I was trying to protect you, Mrs. Tazelaar—get it out of your house so that you would never be involved, would never find out what its contents were. These people know when somebody's lying, and you wouldn't have been if you told them at some point that you had no idea where it was."

"But why didn't you just stop by and ask if I'd found it?"

"I had to be sure. I had to know. If you *had* stumbled upon it, well, this ride would have taken place already."

"Even if I had been unwilling to go along?"

"If you hadn't, you would have been dead in a very short period of time!"

That answer chilled Heather momentarily into silence.

"Why should either of us believe that you *and* our husbands were involved in whatever was going on?" Becky asked.

"Actually I wasn't involved, Mrs. Huizinga, at least, not at the beginning. Nick and Douglas came to me later. They felt someone else had to know, someone who would be what you might call a silent partner. If anything happened to them, I would have all the information that they did. I would be prepared to blow the whistle, as the expression goes."

"How long have you known about Operation Paperclip and the rest of it?" Heather asked finally, though her insides were still trembling from the cumulative effect of all that had happened during the past twenty-four hours.

"Only a few weeks before Nick's death was reported," he told her, an odd expression on his face.

"You seem uncomfortable," Becky observed. "Is there more going on than was contained in the file?"

Weatherby nodded.

"A great deal, Mrs. Huizinga. What Nick and Douglas uncovered was a large part of the story, but not *all* of it."

"What else could there be?" Heather asked.

"You would find what you know so far to be Sunday school material compared to the overall scope."

"Don't tease us, Mr. Weatherby," Becky growled, reacting to pain from her shoulder, which she had to admit he had been able to dress quite expertly, the bullet having passed through the fatty part of her shoulder and out the other side. "We deserve to know as much as you do."

She glanced momentarily at the luggage that Weatherby

had carried from her house and placed beside Heather's own in the living room, four designer suitcases in all, packed with clothes and toiletries and other items literally thrown in because he had succeeded in impressing upon them both the absolute need to get ready as soon as possible.

"The men from Operation Paperclip have been a demonic influence for nearly the past half century," he told them. "Many are dead, but their successors are every bit as corrupt as they are."

"You sound really paranoid," Becky added. "I don't buy paranoia, just fact. Douglas taught me to throw out 90 percent, maybe more, of what someone such as yourself would say. Let's just get to that remaining 10 percent now, or we're not stepping one inch out of this house with you, sir!"

"Have you ever heard of Edgewood Arsenal?" Weatherby asked with apparent reluctance.

"Vaguely," Becky replied, turning to Heather for a reaction. "Sound familiar to you?"

"Something about psychochemical experiments being conducted secretly by the Army?" Heather recalled.

"Precisely. The team of so-called scientists who happened to be in charge of that operation at Edgewood, Maryland, were the very ones who had *developed* quite similar experiments conducted by the Nazis on countless numbers of helpless Jewish and gypsy concentration camp inmates."

"You mean, the sort of thing that Mengele has been condemned for over the years?" Becky asked, deeply disturbed.

"Precisely," Weatherby replied, contempt in his voice.

He looked at them both, his forehead covered with perspiration that had started to drip down past his eyebrows and onto his cheeks.

"While supposedly cooperating with the Jewish community

61

internationally in its search for Mengele, certain Pentagon insiders were also directly in contact with that man, if he ever can be called that.

"This was why Mengele could live as well as he did in Argentina and his various other hideouts, strangely untouched despite the substantial efforts of Simon Wiesenthal and others, and why he is now being given topflight medical treatment in a secret location in Kauai, Hawaii."

His tone was so determinedly matter-of-fact that the significance of what he had just told them almost escaped both.

. . . He is being given topflight medical treatment.

"Mengele is still alive?" Heather said, nearly shouting.

"Josef Mengele of Auschwitz infamy has been a valuable member of Operation Paperclip for a very long time. He is in his early eighties now and has suffered from a heart condition in recent years.

"It was when I found out about this monstrous business, a shocker that Nick and Douglas themselves were so close to uncovering, that I decided to risk everything I have to do something about it."

"But how could this be?" Becky asked, reeling from the emotional impact of such information. "What has happened to a country that can bring itself to tolerate this kind of thing?"

"It is *not* the country as a whole," Weatherby took pains to point out. "It is, rather, pockets of unredeemed Nazis who are themselves manipulated puppets playing their part in a much bigger conspiracy that *could* be exposed very quickly and the perpetrators thrown into jail if it weren't for one thing."

He took out his wallet and held in front of them three twenty-dollar bills, a ten, and several ones.

"It's money, profit. This is the obsession that drives them all, not politics, for most are as apolitical as anyone can be," he said. "The arms merchants are financing a large chunk of the costs of Paperclip, along with other activities of which I've discovered only the vaguest hints, but know enough to make me ashamed of certain elected and other officials.

"And I'm not just talking about those scum who sell vast numbers of rockets and rifles and missile launchers. Unfortunately, this country and a host of others have enormous stockpiles of deadly chemicals that were supposed to have been used in some future war.

"All over the world, these substances are stored improperly in containers that are deteriorating daily, raising the risk of leaks in Russia, France, Germany, England, the United States, and elsewhere.

"The men I'm accusing now once made billion-after-billion from this one kind of weapon alone, a weapon that will probably never be used against any enemy, but which could cause unparalleled havoc if it leaks out into the soil, the water, and the atmosphere."

"Mr. Weatherby," Heather asked, "why did President Kennedy die? The file suggests a conspiracy of everyone from a mafia godfather to the Cubans to who knows what other group!"

"The file is a collection of fact as well as speculation," he replied. "I will add that most of that speculation is probably accurate."

Weatherby cleared his throat, betraying to Heather and Becky how nervous he was.

"Kennedy was about to pull the United States out of Vietnam," he started to tell them.

"That's a well-known theory," Becky interrupted impatiently. "It's been repeated more than once."

"And is quite true, I assure you. When the arms chieftains learned of what he was planning—"

It was Heather's turn to interrupt.

"But how did they? It must have been a highly secret matter. Were you able to trace the source of any leaks?"

"You bet I was!" he replied. "I discovered that the leaks came from two men who were later connected with the House of Representatives banking scandal a couple of years ago. Chicanery had been a pattern with them for a long time. Finally, though, they came to us."

"But what made them do that?" Heather asked.

"They were running scared from greedy political figures who didn't want their misappropriation of taxpayer monies found out. The two I mentioned had gained the reputation of being political whores, selling out to whoever could pay their price. Certain politicos were worried about what might be leaked to the media *this* time."

"Are you saying that they were more afraid of members of Congress than—?"

She interrupted herself this time when she saw the expression of confirmation on Weatherby's face.

"Where you have government," he said, "you have the Internal Revenue Service. And you have, frankly, the FBI, the Secret Service, the National Security Agency, and others. A veteran politician can cause any American citizen almost unimaginable havoc if he were to start feeling threatened."

A car horn honked once outside.

"It's here," Weatherby said.

"Where are we going after the doctor tends to Becky?" asked Heather.

"To the mountains," he said.

"For how long?" Heather demanded.

"Until we can figure out what to do with you."

"We?" Becky asked apprehensively.

"Yes, men and women like myself who are willing to risk their own lives as well."

"Why can't we just stay here, with the house heavily guarded?" Heather asked. "Surely whoever it is wouldn't dare to try anything in such a typical residential neighborhood."

"It isn't as typical as you seem to think," Weatherby told her in an ominous tone. "I suspect you'd be astonished at the truth."

Heather could feel her heart beating faster, her own body drenched suddenly in cold perspiration.

. . . it isn't as typical as you seem to think.

"What are you saying?" she asked.

"No time to explain," he remarked, as he stood.

"That's not good enough," Heather said, angered. "I'm beginning not to like you again, Mr. Weatherby."

"I'll have to live with that," he said coldly. "So will you, Mrs. Tazelaar, if you expect to *stay* alive!"

Dr. Myles Gray was not at all happy about receiving them in the middle of the night.

"I should charge the agency triple time for this," he growled as he let the three of them in, while the driver waited outside in the car.

"Go ahead," Weatherby replied. "You deserve every penny."

"You always did know how to shut me up," Dr. Gray told him.

"Money and women."

"In that order, please!"

He examined Becky, finding that her wound needed some antiseptic and just three stitches.

"Are you in a hurry?" he asked with some sarcasm, then added quickly, "Don't say a word, Karl. I know the answer. The hour somehow gives me just the slightest of clues."

Dr. Gray was quite short, thin, with a small mustache, and wore wire-rimmed glasses. His manner softened as he looked directly at Becky.

"I *can* do this work here without difficulty," he said. "There will be some pain, obviously. But you are very fortunate, ma'am. The bullet did not do the damage that it *could* have done. This is one case, if I might say so, when your weight was advantageous!"

Becky nodded as she told him, "Dr. Gray, no pain now could be any worse than what I've experienced over the past year or so."

He smiled as he patted her on the other shoulder.

"I would like to give you a modified local anesthetic," he said. "It won't be as effective as completely knocking you out, but you won't have to spend hours coming out of it either."

He turned to Heather and Weatherby. "Leave!" he snarled. "I have work to do."

Becky took the brief surgery quite well.

"This man's good," she said, looking only a little pale, but otherwise fine. "He has quite a manner with fat people."

"Yes, that reminds me," remarked Dr. Gray, "your weight could be a problem as time passes. What *are* you going to do about it?"

"Somehow I think food will be secondary over the next few weeks," she said, smiling at him.

"Good!" he commented. "You really are an attractive woman, Mrs. Huizinga. If you lost fifty pounds, you'd be amazed at how much better you would feel *every* day!"

Becky's eyes widened as a very recent and awful image resurfaced in her mind.

"The bodies!" she said. "We were in such a mindless hurry that we forgot about the bodies. They're exactly where we left them."

"You're not the problem, Mrs. Huizinga," Weatherby said. "I am. I'm trained *not* to forget this sort of thing. It was just plain sloppiness. You're not the professional. I'm the one who's supposed to be!"

He was biting his lower lip, obviously worried. "Myles, can I borrow one of your cars?" he asked.

"Sure," the doctor replied. "Take the Caddy—no, the Olds. It's parked in the driveway." A wry smile formed on his face. "I don't trust you with my Caddy." He reached into his pants pocket and tossed Weatherby a set of keys.

Weatherby thanked him, then took Heather and Becky to the car.

"I need to introduce you to our driver. On our way over, there was so much to explain, and there wasn't proper time for introductions. This is Philip," he said. "Philip Spieler. He's an agent like myself—part of our group."

"Group?" Heather asked. "What group is that?"

"Men who are disgusted by the influence of those involved with Paperclip, who consider it a cancer that has spread throughout this country!"

"Are you going back to the house?"

"Yes, I am. I've got to remove those two bodies. I can't get to one of my men soon enough to do it. I'll try to meet up with you at the site."

Weatherby turned to Spieler.

"Factor in half an hour," he said, "and no longer. If I'm not here, leave without me. I'll try to meet you at the copter site. I'd be happier if we could go together, one more gun against the bad guys, in case there is some trouble along the way. But keeping those bodies away from detection is also important. I want the Paperclip crowd to be puzzled by the disappearance as long as possible."

After dragging the two bodies to a crawl space under the Tazelaar house, Karl Weatherby headed back to Dr. Myles Gray's office, checking the rearview mirror in his car more than once to see if there was any indication that he was being followed.

None.

He glanced at his watch a dozen times. When half an hour had passed, he was still a couple of miles away from his destination.

Finally, sweating from head to foot, he pulled up in front.

His fellow agent's car was gone.

I told him to leave in exactly half an hour, he thought with some regret. *I'd better head on out to the—*

The driver's side door of Myles Gray's Caddy, parked in front, was open.

Odd, Weatherby told himself. *He's not usually as forgetful as that.*

He got slowly out of the Olds and approached the driveway.

Blood.

On the pavement.

As though his friend had been hurt and then *dragged* back to the office.

More blood on blades of grass across the side lawn, enough of it to make him think that the cut or whatever Myles Gray had sustained was serious.

The office door was locked.

After pulling out his gun and holding it ready, Weatherby pressed his shoulder against the door, forcing it open. He reached for the light switch and flipped it on.

Everything was as neat as Gray had always kept it. The examination room seemed immaculate, nothing out of place, the waiting room cheerful and tidy with its faintly Hawaiian motif.

Straight ahead was the doctor's private inner office.

Weatherby hurried to the door, knocked three times, then opened it, the familiar odor of aged leather apparent. He tried the light switch to his left, but nothing happened.

After opening the door and walking inside, he saw that the doctor's desk chair had been overturned, the contents of file drawers scattered over the floor. On top of the desk were Myles Gray's glasses, one lens badly cracked.

"Even you!" Weatherby said out loud. "You knew so little!"

"But still too much for him to stay behind—to lead an unrestricted normal life," a deep voice rumbled across the room, spinning Weatherby around on his heels in shock. "It's a pity we didn't arrive sooner. He said the two women had just left. At least we got the good doctor. We can get any information we want from him, then dispose of his body where even hotshots like you will never find him!"

Weatherby glimpsed a very large man standing to one side, the sheer bulk of his body taking up an entire corner of the room.

Opposite him, on the other side of the doorway, were two other men, quite tall, muscular, each holding a gun with a silencer on it.

Karl Weatherby was dead by the time the third bullet hit him.

9

★ ★ ★

They were still driving at sunrise.

"Ever since the beginning of time," Heather mused out loud, thinking of those desperately missed occasions when she and Nick would go jogging together at a similar hour, as much for what they would see around them as for the exercise itself, "it's been so pure and beautiful, painted by God Himself. When my husband would witness a really fine sunrise, he would be driven to tears most of the time. But then he had to pull himself away, to leave that moment and then return to quite another kind of reality."

"All of us have been down that road again and again," Philip Spieler commented, with some sensitivity. "It's tough, God knows how tough, to see beauty of any kind and then have to wallow in the dirt."

He fell silent briefly, as though collecting his thoughts.

"You've had it rough because of the treacherous men behind all this," he added, "but, believe it or not, you're soon going to meet someone who just might have a story to tell that is as tragic as yours."

"Who is it?" she asked.

"A lady named Estelle."

"Why should we meet her?"

"You're both going to need protection as a result of what's happened. If we can get the two of you into hiding and keep you there securely, it'll be better all around. You just might find Estelle to be a fascinating individual. I personally felt as though *nothing* I had ever complained about over the years held even a fraction of the significance and the heartache that she has endured."

Heather studied this man for a moment. He was bigger, broader than Karl Weatherby, who seemed rather slight in comparison. His surfer-boy blond hair capped a face that was porcelain smooth, with blue eyes that seemed so vibrant she half suspected he wore special contact lenses.

"You're quite young," she said. "Are you quite new to the agency?"

"A couple of years now, ma'am," he answered matter-of-factly.

"You risk a great deal."

"For a real good reason."

"Could I ask what it is?"

"My great-grandfather died as the esteemed Wernher von Braun stood by fifty years ago in Germany, with his cronies by his side, and watched the effects of an experiment on him."

Heather didn't know what to say at first.

Spieler sensed her awkwardness and added, "He wasn't a Jew, but just someone who had not pledged his unfettered devotion to the Third Reich as convincingly as the Nazis desired. Because of that, this wonderful man was selected as a guinea pig for some weightlessness experiments that had been

72

devised by von Braun himself, without regard for the human misery to be caused."

He turned his head for a second or two, and those eyes of his seemed to cut right through Heather.

"You know what happened?" he asked.

"You don't have to tell me," she assured him, increasingly sure that it would be traumatic for both of them.

"I want to, it helps, truly it does, you know . . . the memories keep coming back. I wasn't there, of course, but I heard from family members who found out, who literally picked up the pieces and did what they could about making sure that he was buried properly."

"And von Braun just stood by?" she asked.

"Yes, he did. In fact, after my great-grandfather was put in this round, metal chamber and the door was slammed shut, von Braun was the one who threw the switch, and when my grandfather's body literally exploded, von Braun pronounced the experiment successful and seemed actually to rejoice over the fact that they had learned more about weightlessness' impact on the human body. With no tears, no regret, no compassion whatever, he ordered two assistants *to dispose of what was left of a poor old man!*"

Heather was amazed that he could still maintain his attention on the road ahead of them, but then she remembered that this was one of the points of the intensive training received by each agent—training aimed at keeping them in control of themselves whatever the circumstances.

"I'm deeply sorry," she said, and indeed was. "I'm sorry you had to go through all this again."

"It happens periodically," he admitted to Heather. "I can't watch movies that show people being dealt capital punishment in gas chambers in this country. I know the rationale behind it. I suspect, if pressed, that some part of me does agree with the necessity, given what criminals are proving to be capable of. But my great-grandfather died so similarly, yet suffering for no reason, no crime, and the man responsible is given a *de facto* pardon by the United States military, side-stepping the Nuremburg prosecution altogether."

"Don't forget Mengele," Becky added. "That devil's still alive, according to the file. He's being taken care of round the clock at American taxpayers' expense, some of whom suffered the most appalling treatment when they were confined at Auschwitz because of him—a heartless creature presently fed by those who run this so-called Christian nation—isn't that a laugh anymore—as well as clothed and *protected* from capture and trial!"

Heather could feel her friend shaking, much like Spieler had done minutes before.

This is what our husbands found out, and why they died, she thought sadly. *Oh, Lord, Lord, Lord!*

Heather settled back as the ride to some unknown destination continued, wondering if her own life would ever return to normal, while sensing sadly that, with Nick gone, no matter what else happened, "normal" probably wouldn't be an option for a very long time.

The black helicopter was waiting in a clearing surrounded by deserted New Jersey pine barrens.

Both women hesitated as they got out of the car.

"We don't know where we're going," Heather said. "We leave whatever was left of our normal lives behind us now. How can we do that just because strangers tell us to do so? How can we just say good-bye?"

Philip Spieler was sympathetic.

"The process began earlier," he said.

"The day our husbands found out what was going on," Becky said, with a tone of great regret. "If Nick and Douglas had never known, none of this would be happening to us right now!"

"But the fact is that Nick Tazelaar and Douglas Huizinga *did* know," continued Spieler. "They were honest men who took the only course of action possible under those circumstances."

"They could have ignored it," Becky quickly pointed out. "They could have pretended somehow that—"

"You knew Douglas better than any of us could have," Spieler said, his manner gentle. "Was turning away *ever* a part of his makeup, Mrs. Huizinga? Would it have been the remotest option?"

Becky shook her head, not wanting to admit this but unable to avoid the truth it embodied.

He turned to Heather.

"Mrs. Tazelaar," he spoke slowly but not coldly, "would Nick have been *capable* of the kind of pretense that would have been necessary?"

"I wish that, just for a moment—," she started to say.

"Are you telling me that just for a moment it would have been wonderful if he had compromised, if he had put aside his ethics and his decency and looked the other way? Isn't that what you're thinking?"

"Yes, *yes!*" Heather shouted, not able to control her emotions any longer. "I know that sounds perfectly awful, but it would have meant that my Nick would still be here, with me, and yet he's not, because he was so principled, so honest. But for a moment of sacrificing his integrity, a moment that would have passed quickly, he would never have been tortured to death!"

Spieler was standing directly in front of her. She leaned forward, as though about to fall, and he put his arms around her.

"Forgive me . . . ," she sobbed.

" 'It is better to live a short while in the warm rays of an honest sun than to spend a lifetime in the chill darkness of a compromised conscience,' " commented Spieler with great solemnity.

She pulled away and looked at him.

"Nick wrote that, as you undoubtedly realize," she said. "He must have known what would happen sooner or later."

"One or two men cannot fight the many-headed monster and expect to survive. They have to be willing to sacrifice."

"For what?" Becky added. "For things to change, for the evil to be rooted out? But has that occurred, Mr. Spieler? Has any of this gotten any better? Can you honestly assure us that this is so? How different are we?" she said with some irony. "Isn't that going to happen to *us* as well?"

"The chances are high that you're right, Mrs. Huizinga," Spieler admitted. "I can't lie to you about this."

And then he added, cryptically, "We *do* have options."

"What about going directly to the president with what has been uncovered?"

"That's one of them," he admitted.

"Why haven't you gone straight to him long before now?" Heather pressed.

"Because three of the members of his cabinet *are* controlled by the interests we've been made aware of."

"Which ones?" asked Becky, her interest rising.

"That's top secret. I shouldn't have told you as much as I just did."

"Nothing gets to the president without being funneled through one or all of them," Heather said. "I learned that much from Nick."

"That gives you both some insight into the enormity of this problem of ours," Spieler replied.

"How about the media?" Becky suggested. "They've never shown any reluctance to shy away from controversy."

"But they can be intimidated. So many chains or conglomerates are on the scene these days. Get to the CEOs of these, and you've killed a story such as this."

"The tabloids!" Becky pressed. "Look at what they've done to at least one political candidate."

"That's dangerous, too," Spieler told her.

"Why?"

"Two of the three biggies are owned by mafioso or Middle Eastern interests that are part of the arms network."

"You're painting a picture of a country completely shackled by criminals," Heather observed.

"The number of these guys who are involved is really quite small. The problem is that they control crucial avenues of communication—to the president of the United States as well as from the mass media to the American public. Furthermore, every drug addict is a potential or actual puppet of theirs," Spieler said forlornly before adding, "and there are many of *them* in government these days."

He paused, then added, "But there is still plenty of hope."

"It doesn't *sound* that way," she added. "Where *do* we turn? Whom can we trust? How can we be safe anywhere?"

Spieler looked at Heather, then at Becky.

"We all are naked before the enemy unless we have the Holy Spirit within us," he said. "If the Lord be for us—"

"Who can stand against us?" the two women finished the familiar verse in perfect unison.

Spieler shrugged his shoulders as he said, with some reluctance, "How does that explain the deaths of your husbands? I ask a question the answer to which I cannot be sure of learning!"

He had an odd expression on his face. Heather saw some hint of thoughts playing across it that were full of melancholy.

"Mr. Spieler, is there something else?" she probed.

His gaze avoided her own, instead shifting to the outlines of surrounding pine trees that were visible in the dissipating darkness of early morning.

"Oh, it's just that while you hear a lot of things in this job, you *suspect* even more, Mrs. Tazelaar," he replied. "Sometimes, there are whispered suspicions, a thread of some idle rumor perhaps, gained from some anonymous source and picked up and spread from agent to agent."

"What does any of that have to do with Nick and Douglas?" Heather asked apprehensively.

"Sometimes what you hear is so strange that your understandable first reaction is to disregard it, to cast it out of your mind as unworthy nonsense that shouldn't be given a moment's consideration."

"Mr. Spieler, you're not making a great deal of sense," Becky told him. "Is there a point to all of this?"

He looked at them both and seemed to want to say something quite profound, but stopped short of this.

"Nothing," he said in a manner that spoke only of evasion.

Just then, the copter pilot shouted out at them, "We've got to be leaving."

Spieler obviously hated the idea of taking off without Karl

Weatherby having joined them. But he couldn't bring himself to disobey a man he admired so very much.

"I would sacrifice my life for the guy," he admitted, a faint smile curling up the sides of his mouth. "That's true, you know. I don't mean to sound so terribly brave or noble, but Karl has a quality only your husbands matched. You both will see what I mean when you get to know him better."

"You're here, now, putting yourself on the line," Heather reminded him. "What more could you be doing?"

Philip Spieler shook his head, not at all sure what he might offer to her as a reasonable answer.

"Now!" the pilot interrupted them again. "There's something on the radar heading this way. We've got to move!"

As their copter rose from the ground, another helicopter was visible to the rear and seemed to be gaining on them.

"They wanted to get us while we were still on the ground," Spieler told them. "Less messy that way, especially in this isolated area."

"How can this be happening?" Becky asked, rising panic in her voice. "I thought there were FAA rules. After all, this doesn't happen to be a war zone in some shell-shocked foreign country!"

"You are correct, obviously," Spieler responded, "but, while you have some idea of how much influence and outright control these people do have, you cannot realize the full extent unless you have seen all the information that I have. That file didn't contain everything, you know."

Their pilot swung away from some ground lights ahead.

"A housing development," he said. "I won't try to knock *them* out of the air while we're near it, but I can't swear to what those guys—"

The answer was immediate.

An object fired from the pursuing copter missed them by only a few feet.

"That was a small missile!" Spieler exclaimed. "And it's heading straight for those houses!"

Seconds later the missile hit, and they could see an instant burst of flame, followed by another.

Both Heather and Becky screamed as they saw what was happening, the fire spreading like a flood down an embankment.

The pilot sent a code red message over his radio.

Finally, after he finished, he said, trembling, "Nothing like this is ever expected. That's why people choose to live in those cozy little communities, away from the crime and the deterioration of the cities. Most were undoubtedly asleep—many never awoke, at least not for more than a few seconds. Men, women, and children gone! When the truth gets out, that it was a rocket of some sort, the assumption will be some foreign terrorist group!"

"How many people are they willing to sacrifice to get us?" Heather asked, nausea gripping her.

"Whatever it takes," Spieler answered honestly. "A dozen, a hundred, whatever the number. Remember, we're dealing with human devils who have been part of the establishment for so long now that they would never stop short of a few lives to keep themselves exactly where they are."

They swung out over the Atlantic Ocean, hugging the Virginia coast.

"I'm going to return fire now," the pilot said. "I have no rockets, though. Just old-fashioned machine guns. That's always going to be part of the problem. The enemy within our boundaries has an arsenal as big or better than our own. The police are finding that out each day, I'm afraid."

The pilot swung the copter around and fired off a volley of shots before swerving to avoid another missile.

The other copter abruptly swerved and retreated, soon disappearing from any visual contact.

"I don't understand it," the pilot said. "Those guys are retreating. How can that be? They had the better armaments. I wonder what's going on."

"Whoever was in charge must have decided that all this aerial combat is literally too much out in the open," Spieler suggested. "By now the air force, the Coast Guard, and probably the FBI have been alerted. There is a limit to what even a shadow government can accomplish so long as it doesn't have *all* the power!"

"Then they *aren't* in complete control!" Heather exclaimed.

"No, they decidedly are not. But they have enough influence still to be as frightening as you could imagine."

"Where are we heading?" Becky asked.

"Hillbilly country, ma'am," Spieler replied. "You won't believe your eyes when we show you what has been languishing there for a very long time!"

Heather pressed him for something more than that mysterious hint.

"Operation Tuskegee," he told her.

"What in the world is that? I thought we were only concerned with the machinations of Operation Paperclip!"

"They're connected—in a strange and awful way."

Heather was about to press him for details when she noticed that the pilot had started the copter on a descent and then pulled it up again.

"What's wrong?" she asked.

"I didn't like what I saw down there," he remarked.

"What was that?" probed Spieler.

"On the control panel here, the radar can detect certain kinds of ground movement and show it via electronic impulses on the screen."

"*Certain* kinds?" Becky interjected. "Like what?"

He turned and looked at her, then the others.

"Like . . . heat-seeking missiles, ma'am."

Erik Stelzfuss sat in his limousine, infrared binoculars pressed tightly to his eyes.

"Any idea where they might be heading?" he asked, a slight wheezing sound to his voice, a periodic product of years of abuse wrought by his enormous weight as well as by the numerous chemical substances he had been ingesting.

"None, sir," stated the young man next to him on the backseat.

"I have to decide whether to wipe all of them out immediately or simply wait in order to determine where they might be going," Stelzfuss pondered out loud. "An interesting choice, I must say."

"I would recommend the immediate option, sir."

"Why is that, Conrad?"

"Because if where they are heading offers them a means of disseminating what they have learned, we could be in for a difficult time. They've never had someone like this Tazelaar broad to help them. She could be a quite sympathetic figure, sir. The president would be more than willing to listen to her, I am sure."

"Yet it could be a command center of some sort, one we should know about as soon as possible."

"And if a command center, as you say, sir, all the more reason to fear what they can accomplish there in terms of reaching the media or whatever else they might have in mind, before we could do anything to stop them."

Stelzfuss's eyes widened in appreciation.

"Conrad, I am very glad you joined us," he said, patting him on the thigh.

"It is an honor to work with you, sir."

"And not just the extras at my residence?"

"Never that, sir, never that!"

The very large man chuckled, for he knew that Conrad was lying, knew that the handsome newcomer to his staff wanted everything that his house and other plush residences like it maintained around the world had to offer: a cache of drugs in each one that seemed like a cornucopia of special pleasures available for the asking, along with the heavily guarded privacy in which to indulge in them or any other desire he wished.

"How well trained you are, Conrad. How well trained."

"I am honored to have learned at the feet of someone like you."

Erik Stelzfuss's great frame shook with laughter at that one.

"Give the order to blow the fools out of the sky!" he said, chortling. "And then we will, shall we say, retire for the rest of this night and as much of the coming day as the occasion warrants."

Conrad reached for a car phone on the partition in front of him. He spoke into the receiver, then hesitated.

"Sir?"

"Yes," Stelzfuss replied.

"It may be difficult to do this."

"To obey my order?"

"Yes—to destroy them just at the moment."

"Why is that, Conrad?"

"Our sources show a commercial airliner coming into the same flight pattern as the copter."

"So what are you saying?"

"That somehow those whom we are after could prove able to avoid being hit by the missile. Unfortunately, this could happen simply because it is sidetracked by the airliner, which is obviously a much bigger heat source. It, not the copter, could end up being destroyed. In the process, we would have gained for ourselves little else but a case of potentially dangerous public outrage."

Stelzfuss impatiently grabbed the phone out of Conrad's hand.

"Obey my order!" he bellowed into it.

Several seconds passed as he listened.

"I care not about the passengers on that airliner," he said. "We desperately need to take the chance. I have a feeling that this woman could be dangerous. *Now do what I say!*"

He handed the phone back to Conrad.

"Do you think me particularly sadistic or cruel?" Stelzfuss asked the young man.

"You do only what is your pleasure, sir."

Erik Stelzfuss smiled broadly as he added, "At any time, with anyone I choose. Do not ever forget that, my young stallion!"

10

★ ★ ★

Their pilot noticed the blurry, yellow-tinged object that had appeared on the radar screen in front of him, precisely duplicating their southwestern course.

"Large," he said. "Approaching quickly . . ."

He checked the coordinates with great care, then sighed wearily and pushed back in his seat, muttering a profanity as he did so.

"What is it, Robert?" asked Spieler.

"We're in the flight path of a jumbo jet!"

"So get out of its way," Becky said.

"Not that simple," the pilot assured her. "A flight path is not like a two-lane highway in the sky. It's wider than that and less defined at the same time. We're going to have to drop a few thousand feet and change direction altogether. My immediate concern is about our fuel supply."

He leaned forward, concentrating on the screen, his attention caught by something else, the movement so swift and unexpected that even Spieler let out a startled yelp.

"Robert—what the devil is wrong?" he asked.

"A heat seeker has been fired!"

"You've got to be off your rocker, Robert. They must see the airliner in their scope as well. I have to believe that they know the possibility—"

He stopped himself.

"You yourself said that they won't allow anything to get in their way," the pilot reminded him.

"Look!" Becky yelled. "I see the jet."

By now they all did.

"We *can* avoid the missile," the pilot said, "because the airliner represents a far more pervasive source of heat."

He turned to the three others.

"We have an awful choice here," he said in a monotone.

"We need to decide something right now," Spieler went on. "If we stay, we have an opportunity to intercept the missile by placing this helicopter directly in its path. Or we can get out of here right now and save ourselves but doom the jet!"

Heather and Becky glanced at one another. Neither had any hesitation about what was right. They gripped one another's hand in mutual reassurance.

"There's no other way," Heather spoke for the two of them. "Do it! Don't let those creeps have the larger victory."

"Robert, it's been decided," Spieler said. "Are you in agreement, friend?"

"I am."

He tracked the path of the heat-seeking missile and maneuvered the copter more directly into its path.

But none of them had counted on the second missile.

The pilot shouted urgently, "Another one's been fired. Somebody's made the decision that we're to be knocked out of the sky, regardless of whatever else they take with us!"

"Let's move then," Spieler shouted. "If we can't save those passengers, we've got to save ourselves after all."

86

In an instant the first heat seeker shot right past them, drawn by the mammoth jetliner, which it hit in the forward section, splitting the plane and sending thousands of pieces of shrapnel in as many directions.

The shock waves caused by that first mammoth explosion, followed by a series of other successively smaller ones, flung the copter from one side to another like a toy in the hands of an angry child.

The second missile, confused by the enormous outpouring of heat from the destroyed jetliner, spun crazily in the air for a moment, not certain of where to strike, then struck the falling rear section of the larger plane, creating a new source of spinning chunks or slivers of twisted metal.

The debris became like small missiles—one of the copter's plexiglass doors shattered. Projectiles from the airliner were sucked into the now unprotected cabin. One slammed against the pilot's forehead, killing him instantly as he was flung toward the back of the cabin. Spieler was sucked out through the open frame where the doors had been.

Along with Heather herself!

Both found that the air bled instantly from their lungs, and they began gasping spasmodically.

Heather nearly lost consciousness, dizziness and nausea sweeping over her. She could only look with appalling futility while Spieler plummeted past, blood spouting from behind his eyes as the sudden pressure hit them, rupturing tiny fragile veins which protested in the only way possible, his head wrenched to one side at the same time with such force that the neck was broken as a result.

All of this took place in a split second. Heather reached out frantically for something solid, anything that she could manage to grab hold of and, groping, her hands closed around the stabilizer bars that jutted out from the bottom of the copter.

The air was filled with debris—clothes, magazines, plastic cups, and such items as suitcases and portable computers—as well as bodies flung from the jetliner. She saw some of their faces as they were swept past her, most of them dead already, only a few alive, crazed with pain, terrified, and soon as dead as the others, either when they hit the ground or collided with heavy objects.

A single little doll dropped into sight, its material singed, torn, then was gone like the child who must have clung to it not long before.

A small burgundy leather attaché case glanced off Heather's shoulder, shooting pain through her arm, and she was about to let go, unable to hold on any longer, as she repeated Nick's name over and over. Then—

A hand grabbed her own.

"My arm, take hold of my arm!" Becky's voice penetrated her ears above the relentless noise of the chaos all around them. Becky felt the throbbing in her bandaged shoulder as she reached out to Heather. "I hooked my foot around the leg of one of the—"

Her voice was cut off as a jagged section of metal wedged in her right shoulder, the pain sending her into unconsciousness.

Heather could not scream, could not allow herself to faint, could do nothing but pull herself up the length of that momentarily still body, the clothes tearing loose, her hands frantically grabbing for a hold on a plump arm, then the large waist.

The odor of gasoline and burning things—plastic materials, human flesh, much more—was suffocating.

No! her mind cried out. *No, Lord, oh, oh Lord, don't let it end like this. I need to find out more about what really happened to Nick! I need to do what I can to stop the devils who were behind his death.*

Heather managed to reach the bottom rim of the doorway, cutting her fingers on the rough metal edges, then, straining even more, she pulled herself inside and, for a few moments, remained there on the copter's floor, her overworked lungs threatening to explode from exertion that made all her aerobics classes over the years seem like the games of children in comparison.

Suddenly the copter lurched, and Becky's foot unhooked from the seat leg. Her body started to slip away from the copter, nearly taking Heather along with it as she grabbed her friend's ankles, whose weight succeeded in wrenching every muscle in her own body.

It could have been a couple of minutes or only a few seconds, but time ceased to matter as she struggled to keep the other woman from falling to her death. Finally, with a strength not her own, she managed to get Becky back into the cabin, then sank to her knees as she tried to get her breath. Heather scanned the control panel of the copter and saw with relief that it had been set on autopilot. She turned her attention to Becky.

A few moments later, Becky regained consciousness.

"Your shoulder," Heather said. "There was some metal wedged in it."

"That's when I blacked out. It's gone now."

"There's a cut but no bleeding," she observed.

"All the pressure outside must have done something to the flow of blood," Becky said weakly. "Closed it right off. . . ."

Another lurching movement, downward this time.

Roger Elwood

Autopilot keeps this bird in the air for a little while, Heather thought, *but it doesn't land the copter.*

Somehow she had to do that herself. With so little experience, she had to try. And yet she realized what a task it seemed.

Lord Jesus, what a miracle that Nick was a pilot, and that he took me up those times in a copter. We thought it was just something fun to do, fun to be in the air like that together. . . . But now it's going to mean a lot more.

She dragged herself to the pilot's seat and glanced with confusion at the instrument panel, remembering very little from that one afternoon.

Heather grabbed hold of the wheel and pulled back on it sharply.

The copter's plunge was momentarily aborted, and it started to fly straight.

She held the control wheel steady, glancing down for a second or two, seeing only patches of flames.

"How do I land, and where?" she said out loud, her mind searching for every tip that Nick had provided that one afternoon.

Suddenly, straight ahead, Heather saw another copter, this one painted green, heading straight for the one she was in.

Her first reaction was that it would ram her if she didn't swerve to one side. But it abruptly changed course and pulled away just before the two copters made contact, hovering above her for a short while.

Heather's first instinct was to turn aside, perhaps to the left, or else slip farther below it, the autopilot hopefully keeping the speed constant.

A rope ladder!

She saw a rope ladder dropping from the other copter and noticed the words U.S. AIR FORCE on the side.

Someone's coming to help. Someone who wants to—

Without warning, shots were being fired at her copter, shots from a semiautomatic rifle held by whoever was on that ladder. The glass bubblelike covering over the interior splintered on the right side.

Heather turned the control wheel sharply in that direction. She heard a single scream, then something hit the side of the copter and apparently bounced off.

The other copter turned sharply and left in an easterly direction.

"Everything's in this wheel," she remembered Nick telling her. *"A lot of other unexpected problems might get in your way— the rotors stalling, the engine catching fire because fuel lines have ruptured, a great deal else, in fact, that could prove fatal—but, my love, barring anything like that, if you have command of this one little wheel, if you use it properly, you are halfway to safety."*

"It's great to know that," she had told him, *"I need advice about driving on the beltway more than about flying any kind of plane."*

"We're always in some kind of danger, you and I," he had added gently. *"I've taught you how to fire a gun, and you accepted the wisdom of that. Trust me, Heather, you never know when certain knowledge will be useful, no matter how off trail it might seem under the present circumstances."*

Nick acted in so positive a manner, as though from some kind of special leading of the Lord, as he would have put it, and so I did pay considerably more attention to what he was telling me. . . .

Heather smiled at the memory of Nick's typically reassuring voice, his hand on her shoulder, his lips on her ear. . . .

Down.

She had to ease the copter down, had to try to land it, had to do *that,* and nothing else, for only this would save her life.

Debris directly below her. Clouds of smoke.

Trees igniting in a stunning, ripplelike movement outward from the site where the jetliner had crashed.

Heather saw a large clearing about a mile or two south of the crash site.

"If only you could see me now," she said. "Oh, Nick—"

"I think both our men would be very proud of us," Becky suggested, her voice a little stronger. "Too bad they aren't—"

A burst of smoke from below obscured Heather's vision for as much as forty seconds. When it cleared, she had temporarily lost sight of the clearing.

There! she thought, relieved, after spotting it again. *Praise God!*

As she approached, she slowly pushed forward on the wheel, and the copter eased down until it had almost touched ground.

A large black automobile burst out of the surrounding trees, and three men immediately jumped from it, each one carrying a machine gun. All of them opened fire at the same time.

Heather pulled back on the wheel, but nothing happened, the blades above her damaged by the gunshots. The copter angled into the ground and nearly ended up on its nose before settling back.

"Go!" Becky snapped. "I'll stay behind, hold them off as long as—"

"How could you expect me to do that?" Heather interrupted. "I won't throw you to the lions!"

The men stopped momentarily, raising their fists in a shout of celebration, and then continued walking toward the still copter, this time without firing.

Both women crouched on the floor, every muscle in their bodies sore, their clothes torn, faces bruised.

As Heather glanced up, she noticed a single, isolated, orange-colored button on the control panel.

The copter's guns, Heather recalled, knowing that the men were not far away, that she had no other option. *That's what the pilot used earlier to drive off the first copter.*

She heard a voice, a deep, coarse voice say, "Be careful. Somebody might be alive. I would not be very happy with any of you if this fails at the last minute and we end up chasing them yet again."

"We know that, sir," another replied. "Nobody's going to be in very good shape in there. Piece of cake, Mr. Stelzfuss! We can handle anyone who may have survived, especially the Tazelaar woman."

Heather pressed the button, which was connected to the triggering mechanism for the guns built into both sides of the copter.

Nothing happened.

"These guns aren't dependent upon its electronic circuitry," Nick had told her. *"This was done in case a copter cannot get off the ground for lack of fuel or damage to its rotors or whatever other reason, because it leaves the pilot with a supposedly independent means of defense that he can use to hold off attackers.*

"But there's a problem, Heather: What always worries me is that anything purely mechanical is susceptible to jamming, and these systems are particularly prone to just that . . . jamming at the worst possible moment. It's another example of arms makers cutting corners to maximize their profits, regardless of the consequences for those the weapons are supposed to protect in the first place!"

She tried again, four times in succession—once, twice, a third . . . then—

The weapons sputtered noisily to life. The three men were sprayed with scores of bullets, dropping them to the ground in seconds, some of the gunfire also hitting the gas tank of the large black automobile, which burst into flames, sending yet more red-hot debris into the air and igniting other trees in that vicinity. The smell of burning rubber and other materials joined that of homes and commercial buildings from miles around, all of it making breathing increasingly difficult over the coming moments as the conflagration spread.

Before Heather passed out from the smoky air and the cumulative shock of what had occurred in so short a period of time, she caught a glimpse of a monstrously heavy man, his clothes on fire, lurching into the surrounding trees, screaming. . . .

11

★ ★ ★

The odor of leaking gasoline awakened Heather Tazelaar.

She was near the empty doorframe. As she opened her eyes, she noticed a large pool of the liquid collecting outside the copter less than a foot away.

All around her the air was tinged with a dull red mist by little orange-red embers that were floating through it, one after the other landing close to the gasoline.

As she tried to raise herself to a sitting position, she felt a sharp pain in her back and had to remain momentarily stationary, her eyes on that puddle, those embers at the very edge, randomly dropping from the air.

"We've got to get out—run for it!" she shouted.

She decided to crawl out, pulling herself forward slowly, too slowly, she knew, but there was nothing else she could do. If her back had been injured, she risked even more severe problems by exerting it too much.

Becky was just inches away, still on the seat in

front of the instrument panel where she had unleashed the helicopter's guns. Her head had been flung backward.

She was moaning.

"We've got to get out of here," Heather said.

Becky's eyes opened.

"You've got to," she gasped. "I . . . I don't matter. They're after you."

"But you know just as much now."

"How can they be sure of that? They can't. You're the target."

"I can't leave you!" Heather screamed.

"You'll have to!" Becky insisted.

Gathering together what strength she had left and ignoring the pain in both her shoulders, she leaned forward and grabbed hold of Heather with her large hands, flinging her out of the cabin.

The copter now rested in a small lake of gasoline. She fell over into it, getting it in her mouth, her nose, her eyes, her ears.

So much like hell, Heather thought. *Everywhere I turn, I see, I sense nothing but pain and—*

She managed to stumble away from the downed copter. It was barely a minute before several of those vagrant embers finally touched the leaked gasoline, igniting it. The explosion was so powerful that Heather was knocked off her feet and thrown against a large tree trunk, more pain lacerating her.

Seconds later she heard a familiar voice yelling to her, "I got out in time, Heather. I—"

She turned to see her friend suddenly confronted by two men.

A struggle.

Heather started to run forward.

"No!" Becky screamed.

Heather obeyed her friend. She ran, sobbing as she did so, moving as fast as she could. There were more embers than ever now, one after the other landing on her gasoline-soaked clothes. She heard *sizzle-sizzle-sizzle* again and again, brushing them off as they touched her.

She entered the surrounding forest, knowing that its overhead branches could both shelter her temporarily from the falling embers and, with little warning, become an inferno that trapped her.

There was nothing else she could do—the clearing had become a virtual furnace, not an inch of it free of flame. As she glanced back, she could see additional trees igniting, the fire spreading outward.

Heather tripped, fell, got to her feet, and ran.

She heard a man's voice, familiar, but she couldn't think clearly enough to place it.

He was in apparent pain. The sound came from directly ahead of her, so faint that she barely heard it.

The trees stopped at a dirt road. A jeep was parked. Men gathered around it. Heather glimpsed a monstrously heavy man . . . his clothes on fire, lurching into the surrounding trees, screaming. . . .

The same one that had ordered the shots to be fired!

His clothes were charred, his face a mass of oozing fluids.

"We can help you, sir," said another man, quite young, bending over him. "Please calm down. It was fortunate that you had the foresight to have us trail the limo just in case anything happened. As usual, you showed—"

"Stop babbling! I will be scarred for life!" the fat one interrupted. "Nothing can be done. How can I be calm?"

A third man, older, tried to assure him, "Please calm yourself. You need to keep from going into shock. Techniques exist now, surely you know that. Mengele can help us."

Mengele!

Heather stifled a gasp. She had assumed recent media reports confirming his death had been accurate.

"Yes, yes, I know," the fat man said grudgingly, his voice strained. "Get him immediately. Make sure Waimea is ready. And take the woman with you."

Becky!

Heather tried to breathe as quietly as possible and to avoid any movement whatever. She knew that what she was hearing was so sensational a revelation that, if it could be released to the media, it would throw the whole clandestine arms industry into turmoil. That one discovery would invariably lead to others, reporters everywhere relishing the bait as they performed their role of journalistic bloodhounds. A story or series of stories that drew together the Kennedys, Josef Mengele, and others would be guaranteed to keep everything from the supermarket tabloids to the *New York Times* going for months!

The fat man was nearly unconscious, shock setting in, as he grabbed the leather jacket of the older man and said, "Whatever else happens, destroy that woman. *Under no circumstances must Heather Tazelaar be allowed to remain alive!*"

She reacted with shock as her name was spoken out loud, carelessly snapping some twigs underfoot.

The fat man had blacked out by then, but the two with him, well trained as they were, heard the sound.

"I'll take Stelzfuss," the older one said. "You go on after whoever that is! Take them out as soon as you can."

Heather ran, her ankles protesting as she stepped on small rocks or the broken, bare ends of fallen branches.

Several times she heard a semiautomatic rifle shoot a stream of bullets directly above her head.

Heather stopped and saw that the trees thinned out, and opened into a ravine with a tiny stream down the middle. Rising high on both sides was a mountain with a sheer, threatening face that she knew Nick, ever the consummate athlete, would have found difficult to scale.

Suddenly the gunfire had stopped.

She hesitated for a moment.

Too long.

A tall, slender, red-haired man sprang out from behind the trees to her left, knocking her down.

Beating her fists at him, she fought back, but he was far stronger and ended up sitting on her midsection, pressing her hands back against the pebble-strewn bed of that stream.

"Stop it, Mrs. Tazelaar!" he yelled at her, veins bulging among the freckles on his forehead.

"So that you can follow those orders whoever it was gave you?" she screamed back. *"Don't bet on it!"*

She bit his left hand and held on for a few seconds before letting go.

He stood and stepped back several feet from her.

"You have a choice," he said. "Run or wait a minute and listen!"

"That's not a choice," she retorted weakly. "You want an excuse so that you can shoot me in the back."

"I would *never* do that to the wife of Nick Tazelaar, under ordinary circumstances," he remarked. "That man's memory deserves better, much better, don't you think? Fat boy Stelzfuss is a more appropriate target for that sort of thing!"

Heather saw the expression on his face and realized, without knowing clearly why, that perhaps she didn't have to run from him after all.

"My name is Patterson," he said as he helped her to her feet. "Your husband organized a special task force that was as secret as anything the agency has ever attempted. Only he and the director knew about it."

"What was the purpose?"

"To infiltrate an organization formed by Erik Stelzfuss— the fat man you saw—and others. Their goal is to sell arms to as many people—and countries—as possible."

Behind them clouds of black smoke grew thicker than ever.

"Surely *this* will blow the lid off Stelzfuss," Heather assumed.

"It probably won't, unfortunately," Patterson told her honestly. "A plane crashing into houses and office buildings is tragic, certainly, but no longer fresh news. It's happened before, though obviously not for the same reasons. The media will do their thing, of course. They may even stay with it for a few days, and then it'll be *made* to disappear. I assure you that *made* is very much the operative word here."

"That's hard to believe," Heather responded, stunned at first, but then uncomfortably suspecting that Patterson may have been correct. "Are you saying that they'd be more inclined to pay attention to a love affair involving, say, a political candidate than anything of this magnitude? Both are wrong, but can they even try to justify a stand that says an international organization spreading terror, blackmail, and who knows what else, is worth *less* coverage?"

"But then don't you find human nature regularly dumbfounding?" Patterson mused. "A hundred years ago, there were no Gay-Pride parades. A hundred years ago, good people didn't find it necessary to demonstrate outside abortion clinics—if they had, they would have been touted as he-roes, not criminals being carted to jail."

"But what about an investigation? I can't believe that the federal government will *ignore* what has happened."

"Sure, sure, there will be that, you can count on it—all very public, with fascinating sound bites instead of any real depth—and there may be some questioning of certain so-called suspicious individuals, but believe this, Mrs. Tazelaar, it will all fade sooner than you'd guess, with nothing accomplished."

"What they count on is the inability of people to be so moved by tragedy that it motivates their behavior after the evening news is over!" Heather said.

"And they're right often enough that they can go on playing their games with some degree of impunity."

Shaken, feeling alone with Nick gone and with Becky suddenly captured, and now with only a stranger to depend upon, Heather started to cry.

"You can cry all you want," Patterson assured her. "But you should avoid staying in this one spot for very much longer. If I am not sufficiently convincing with the people around Stelzfuss, then they'll come right after you again."

"What can you do about Becky?" she asked, getting her emotions under control again. "Can you help her stay alive?"

"I'll do what I do. But listen, there's something else I should tell you. If you meet a woman named Estelle . . . listen to what she has to say."

"One of your agents who was with me on the copter mentioned her name. Where is she likely to be?"

"At a shopping mall near here. It's the only one. This is a poor area that can't support any others. I hope the two of you can make contact."

"What does she have to say?" Heather demanded. "It all sounds so mysterious."

"It's too involved to tell you now, under these present conditions." He cleared his throat and went on. "Listen up. This is far more important just now. Here's what I'll do: I'm going to fire a succession of shots. And I'll tell them that you're dead. Hopefully that will cause them to stop searching for you, unless the fat boy himself needs to see an actual corpse in order to be placated."

"What will you do then?" she asked, sniffling.

"That won't be a problem. We can achieve a lot with reconstructive surgery and make a corpse look like almost anyone we want."

She smiled as she reached out and shook hands with him.

"I'm sorry I was so hard to convince," she said, embarrassed. "What do I do now? Where do I go, Mr. Patterson?"

"Less than a mile ahead, you'll come to a fork in the stream. If you turn left, you'll soon reach a very small village. Ask for Elijah. That's where you would have been by now if your helicopter hadn't been intercepted."

"Is Elijah an agency operative?"

"In a manner of speaking, yes."

"What will be there in that village for me?"

"Leftovers from the Tuskegee Project."

"Nick had something to do with it, didn't he?"

"Your husband uncovered the truth. That was another reason for his death. . . . I must go now, Mrs. Tazelaar. My prayers go with you."

"And my own with you."

Heavenly Father, prayer is all we have left, she thought.

Patterson took his pistol from its holster under his right arm.

"Go, Mrs. Tazelaar, go now!" he urged her.

She started running.

What if he's lying? she asked herself. *What if he's just going to aim that weapon at me and shoot me in the back?*

As the first shot rang out, echoing off the surrounding mountainsides, her muscles stiffened, waiting for some pain to set in.

"I'm not going to shoot you!" Patterson yelled after her. "This isn't a trick. Please . . . run!"

Three more shots were fired.

As Heather continued running, she examined the scene directly in front of her.

On either side, rugged mountain peaks formed an impressive barrier to the outside world, the stream slicing equidistantly through them. Any village such as the one Patterson spoke of must have been built right up against those two walls of stone, keeping the inhabitants extremely remote for any number of years.

Elijah, here I come, she told herself as she slowed down and started walking along the right side of the creek.

But where did it start? How much farther would she have to go beside the stream before she found—

She glanced back over her shoulder.

He was gone.

Everyone she could turn to had been taken from her life. Every familiar sight was somewhere else, seemingly out of reach, and she was now hurrying toward an uncertain destination and a meeting with a complete stranger.

Finally, out of breath and not watching her steps, she tripped over a rock and fell into the stream, twisting her ankle.

Something fell on her cheek. She wiped it off and looked at her fingers.

Ash.

Carried by a breeze that was tracing its way between the mountain peaks. More pieces were now visible in the air.

She inhaled several of these, which made her sneeze and then cough violently, her lungs and stomach muscles hurting now along with her ankle.

Heather tried to stand but her ankle would not tolerate this, and she fell again, scraping her right knee.

A moment later, she saw the cougar.

She sensed the animal at first, intuition or whatever warning her that she was being stalked.

As it jumped from a hidden perch to the streambed, she was alerted by the sound of rocks or pebbles that it had moved.

Thirty feet to her right, crouching low, its whiskers and ears flattened, its upper lip pulled back, its eyes locking in on her like the heat-seeking missile earlier had done with the jetliner.

No weapons.

She had nothing except stones.

The cougar seemed bloated, yet very hungry, though she couldn't imagine why, since that area appeared to be likely territory for plenty of game.

Pregnant!

It was a she-cat, expecting a litter, and hunting down some food. If it had come upon a rabbit or a deer, the reaction would have been the same.

Heather stayed as immobile as she could manage. For a minute or so, the cougar seemed content to do nothing but study her. Then it moved forward a few feet.

She screamed—the worst thing she could have done, because it showed fear—and this only emboldened the cougar. It ran ahead, but stopped again. This time it was less than a dozen feet from her.

She searched for the largest rock within reach and picked it up. Somehow she managed to stand by putting her weight on her uninjured leg, though she was unsteady at best.

The cougar sprang. Heather swung the rock at it. She connected not with its head but its right shoulder, and it let out a cry of pain or rage or both, landing not more than five feet from her.

Heather was dazed. The three-hundred-pound animal had wrenched her insides when it collided with her. And falling back against the hard, sharp rocks along the stream had cut and bruised her.

She was gasping, trying to get her breath back. The cougar was doing the same thing.

Heather stood again, though even more uncertainly than a moment ago. This caught the mountain lion's attention and it, too, got to its feet, but with more balance than she had.

She stumbled back, without falling. The cougar advanced toward her.

Play dead. . . .

Those words from some childhood game rose to the surface of her mind, with no memory of the context.

She deliberately fell this time, sending more needles of pain throughout her body. Then she remained utterly without movement, trying not to breathe.

The cougar stood like a carved wildlife statue for a moment, sniffing the air, its hunger taunted by the odor of fresh meat, a large tongue licking its lips.

It approached her still body with great caution, its wet nose pressed up against soft, bare, human skin, that tongue tasting the surface.

Then the cougar closed its large mouth around Heather's right wrist and started shaking it. Heather had to stifle any normal instinctive reactions such as pulling away, or screaming again.

Satisfied for the moment, the animal approached her head.

Its breath was warm against her face, its whiskers tickling her lips, her nose, and she prayed that this wouldn't make her sneeze.

And then it let out an abrupt cry of pain and plopped down next to her.

Heather could not guess how much time passed. She had no watch, no way of telling the minutes. She passed out once, and when she came to again, she saw something quite amazing under the circumstances.

The cougar had crawled about fifteen feet away, apparently trying to find some sort of shelter. But its strength had failed. As it was resting there on a rough bed of stones, this mother was giving birth.

Heather was able to stand, but no more steadily than before. She knew she had a chance to get away if she didn't hurt herself anymore. Gingerly she started to turn, then stopped as the mother cougar let out a strange and awful roar.

She could just barely glimpse five tiny, blind, wet forms beside their mother. None were moving.

Raising itself a bit, the cougar roared again, in the same manner, then fell back against the stones.

Get out, stupid, she told herself. *If that cat revives, you'll—*

The cougar was dead.

Heather saw that as she approached. And so were the five little ones . . . all of them stillborn.

A little like me, she thought, *trying to survive in the only way she knew how!*

"You were really fortunate!" an exuberant voice proclaimed loudly, repeating itself in an echo.

Heather, startled, turned, and saw a tall, stocky, white-haired black man, a rifle in his hands, walking toward her.

"Are you Elijah?" she asked weakly.

"I am, that I am," he said, smiling broadly.

She collapsed in his arms.

12

★ ★ ★

Heather Tazelaar regained consciousness as unfamiliar cooking odors reached her nose—rich, vibrant scents of whatever-it-was being prepared.

She opened her eyes, saw that she was inside a bare, shacklike building, and felt a soft mattress beneath her.

An ancient-looking, thin-faced black woman sat beside her, holding her left hand—after a fashion at least.

No fingers.

The old woman had only little stumps instead.

"My name's Ophelia," she said. "Terrible looking, ain't they?"

Heather's face flushed red.

"I'm sorry. Forgive me for staring."

"That's fine, Heather. Don't you be concerned, ma'am. Most people do the first time—stare, that is."

"You know my name?"

"We've been told a lot about you. Your husband—"

Heather pushed herself up to her elbows.

"You met Nick?" she asked, startled.

A smile crossed Ophelia's face.

"He came here just a few weeks ago."

A few weeks!

"He died soon afterward," Heather mumbled, unable to restrain her emotions. "In Germany . . . near Düsseldorf."

The old woman's expression became serious.

"That's what they say, yes, it sure is," Ophelia remarked ominously as she avoided any eye contact.

Heather's palms started sweating.

"You spoke strangely just then," she pointed out. "What's wrong?"

Ophelia seemed ready to answer when Elijah came in.

"How are you getting along?" he asked cheerfully.

Heather smiled as she said, "Glad to be alive, Elijah."

"Let's get some food into you," he remarked. "See to it, please, Ophelia. We'll be back shortly."

The old woman stood slowly and walked over to a stove that seemed as old as she was.

"Do you feel like coming outside, Mrs. Tazelaar?" Elijah asked.

"That would be good," Heather told him.

He helped her to her feet. As she was walking toward the front door, the only door in that one-room structure, she noticed that Ophelia was wearing no shoes, her feet in much the same condition as her hands.

Once outside, Heather asked Elijah what had happened.

"She's a Tuskegee guinea pig," he said, "just like the rest of us."

She had no idea what he was talking about.

"It's something else your husband stumbled onto, ma'am,"

Elijah told her. "Something that came right out of Operation Paperclip."

Heather glanced over her surroundings, which seemed to offer a typical slice of Appalachian life. The homes were small and ramshackle, mostly covered by rusty tin roofs . . . murky water in puddles on both sides of the dirt street . . . an odor that was a mixture of human waste and burning wood from stoves.

The people were different, though at first glance they also appeared to be like those living elsewhere among the mountain communities of West Virginia and surrounding states . . . in this case black, with shabby, torn clothes, some trudging through pockets of mud in their bare feet.

Black, poor, and deformed.

Heather had walked only a short distance before she had to stop. A little girl was walking past her, a little girl born without eyesockets.

"Your husband reacted the same way," Elijah told her.

She could picture Nick doing that, his legs frozen, tears coming at full flow, his stomach tightening, his lungs barely able to inhale.

"Welcome to the U.S. government's version of hell," Elijah added.

The ones with missing toes and/or fingers were the more fortunate of those she saw. Some were grotesquely retarded, with protruding foreheads so extreme that she could not look at them for more than a second or two. Others had been born with no limbs at all and were propped in simple high-backed wooden chairs as they looked with despair at the world that was theirs.

"What happened?" she asked, her voice hoarse. "What was done to all of these people to make them like this?"

"Them German scientists from Operation Paperclip seemed *anxious* to become involved with the Tuskegee Project almost from the start of it," Elijah replied. "They were not able to use Jews any longer, so they grabbed some black folk like these and lied to them in order to get their agreement to allow the experiments."

"What experiments are you talking about, Elijah? And you? I don't see anything wrong with you."

"If I don't take my medicine, it'll become obvious soon enough."

Elijah took Heather into three homes, where she saw people who were blind, like the child she had just seen, and others who had lost their sight much later in life.

"The so-called medicines," he told her, "prescribed by Tuskegee doctors were designed, they said, to test the effects of certain drugs on pressure within the eyes. In just about every case, ma'am, it caused inoperable glaucoma, which advanced far more rapidly than anyone had suspected."

"But the babies I'm seeing," she asked, "the ones born without eye sockets? How did something like that happen?"

"Their mothers took the drugs."

"While they were carrying their unborn child?"

"Yes. . . ."

It reminded her of what had happened during the thalidomide nightmare of the late fifties and early sixties.

"Thalidomide," she asked. "Was that involved, Elijah?"

He turned away sadly and headed out the front door.

Once outside, Elijah remarked, "The blind ones can't see all this around them, of course. That much is a blessing for them. But they can *smell* it all, they can *hear* the moaning, the cries of other children whose mothers' genes were damaged by Tuskegee drugs."

112

"Generation after generation affected," Heather mused, "for endless decades to come. Like the effects of radiation exposure."

"There ain't no doubt about that, ma'am," he agreed.

They walked up the street to another home at the opposite end.

"My place," Elijah said simply.

It was pretty much a duplicate of the others, with its rusty tin roof atop a frame of old wood, some of it rotted through or mangled by termites. There was no one inside. Heather saw faded old photographs of a woman and several children.

"All dead now," Elijah told her. "I held my wife in my arms as she coughed herself to death. Her lungs had ceased to function. Her arteries were hardened long before they should have been. I could get no doctor to come."

"What sort of response have you gotten when you've petitioned the Feds for help?" Heather asked.

"Form letters in return," the old man told her wearily. "Those behind the Tuskegee Project have sealed off any real contact with anyone who might be a little sympathetic to what we've been facing."

"But the federal bureaucracy is so big. How could—?"

"And all you have to do is to have one of your guys in charge of the mailroom," he interrupted. "It's as simple as that."

That astonishing truth hit Heather hard. "But what about calling someone—a senator, for example? Haven't you done that?"

"We have no phones."

"None at all?"

"Pay phones near the main highway, but they never work."

He smiled a bit but not with any joy.

"We've been isolated like this for a very long time, ma'am."

"My husband was here last year?" Heather asked.

Elijah nodded.

"But I didn't see anything in the file he had found that even suggested that this Tuskegee Project was in existence."

"It was on a TV program, ma'am. A news program."

"Did it talk about the involvement of former Nazi war criminals?"

"The project itself. They didn't have the guts to tell the rest."

"And Nick made a connection?"

"What he told me was that it seemed like other cases he had found."

"The experimentation with the effects of nerve gas on soldiers who had volunteered unwittingly?"

"I think you got it right."

"The same men!"

"From Germany to the United States. While they are trying Göring, Rosenthal, and others, many are being *welcomed* into this country."

"And the financing comes from the arms cartel?"

"Yes. . . ."

"But what's the connection? What do they get out of it?"

Elijah had to sit down abruptly in an old rocking chair.

"The drugs they used became part of what they sold . . . along with their missiles and the rest. That Hussein guy in the Middle East bought truckloads of the stuff and is ready to use it when he senses the right moment."

"Germ and chemical warfare!" Heather exclaimed.

"Yes, that's what it is, but we were treated like *the enemy* a quarter of a century ago," the old man said. "We're so dumb, we're like lambs that they slaughtered, but without a knife. It's a slower death, worse for all of us."

Elijah's eyes were suddenly bloodshot and watery, his breathing becoming heavier and heavier, all strength seemingly leaving him as his hands fell to his sides and his shoulders slumped.

"My medicine," he told her as he pointed. "On the table . . . over there . . . one pill. . . . Please hurry!"

Heather saw the dark-yellow plastic bottle with a white snap-on cap, rushed over and grabbed it, frantically flipping off that cap and tapping out a single tiny pill in her left hand.

"No water," Elijah mumbled, "no time."

He opened his mouth, and she slipped him the pill. He had started shaking, and she was forced to hold his mouth shut. After a couple of minutes, he became calm again.

"Does something with my metabolism . . . ," the old man acknowledged. "But . . . but it's not . . . it's not—"

Suddenly Elijah pressed both hands to his forehead and fell over in front of her on the dirt floor.

She bent down, felt his pulse.

He was still alive.

A moment later, his eyes fluttered open. "It comes and goes," he said weakly. "Someday it will be too much for me, and I will leave this place of misery. How I yearn for what the Lord has promised . . . another life free of pain and sorrow."

13

★ ★ ★

The following morning, an hour or so after dawn, Ophelia delivered a halting, rambling, but soul-deep eulogy for a Tuskegee victim who had died during the night, the entire several-score-strong population of the village gathering around the primitive grave-site, which was located in a section of others, each marked by a makeshift wooden cross.

"We have no way of preserving bodies here," she explained as she and Heather sat on the front porch of her home. "And the humidity is often so awful that we have fallen into the habit of getting the funeral over with as soon as we surely could."

"It seems so unbelievable that they could get away with this," Heather remarked. "And yet I've been seeing the proof right out in front of me."

"We're not alone here, you know," the ancient black woman told her. "There are places like this all over the country. They come every so often to monitor us, to offer platitudes about our nonexistent care, and to throw a few bundles of food in front of us, thinking that that is all they owe us."

That was another truth Heather had not realized. That these places of poverty and illness were kept hidden from media scrutiny, not out of any concern over the political embarrassment as such that the victims represented, but because *the experiment had never really ended.*

Heather thought of Nick then, of all that he had known for weeks or longer before he died.

"It's really amazing that my husband was able to keep everything from me," she admitted.

"He knew it all," Ophelia said. "He knew about the Creoles in Louisiana and the Sioux out west and the hippies—"

"All part of the experimentation?"

"Them and others . . . the soldiers who volunteered . . . the old folks who had no idea what was going on. . . . Sheep to the slaughter, Mrs. Tazelaar."

She was about to say something else when a loud noise interrupted her.

"They're coming," Ophelia said ominously.

"At this time of morning?"

"Anytime it pleases them."

The sound was that of a medium-sized truck.

"You've got to hide," Ophelia stated the obvious. "You're not black and you don't look poor."

"But where?" she asked.

"There's a tunnel in the mountain. It's in back of my house. Bushes cover it. Don't go too far back. Stay at the entrance."

Don't go too far back.

The words chilled her, and she asked what they meant.

"Tarantulas," Ophelia said. "Maybe a hundred of them, maybe more. They have their nests farther on in the tunnel. They come into this little place of ours in droves sometimes."

"And people die?"

"From fear, not from the tarantulas themselves."

118

"Aren't they poisonous?"

"Sure they are. But only the African kind are deadly. These hurt no more than a common bee sting, Mrs. Tazelaar."

"That's comforting."

Ophelia chuckled. "Don't bother them and they won't hurt you, even a little."

Heather followed her to where the tunnel began.

"Our visitors still might find you, but I doubt it," Ophelia told her. "I come and get you when it's safe."

About six feet high and nearly as wide, the tunnel was damp inside from humidity, and it smelled of great age. The odor in fact was nearly overpowering, and Heather started to sneeze and cough.

She could see nothing, could only hear voices outside. Bits and pieces of sentences, including a name: *Stelzfuss*.

She swallowed hard, her heart pounding faster at mention of the man.

He should be dead . . . he was covered by flame . . . he should be—

A shot rang out.

She pushed some branches aside, peered out, got a truncated view between Ophelia's house and the one next to it. People were being beaten, clubbed. A tall, broad-shouldered man dressed in army fatigues had Ophelia by the neck and was dragging her somewhere.

Heather couldn't let this continue. Saving the entire community was impossible, but freeing that one ancient black woman had to be attempted.

She found a large tree branch on the ground at the tunnel's entrance. Grabbing it, she ran up to the man. Startled, he dropped Ophelia and reached for a large knife holstered in his belt.

119

Heather swung the branch, wrenching her shoulder as she did. It connected solidly at the side of his neck. He groaned once, then fell.

Heather hurried to Ophelia's side.

"I'll help you stand," she whispered.

"I can't . . . too much pain . . . ," the woman responded, her voice hoarse.

"You've got to get out of here."

"Where do I go? It's the same everywhere. They control the world. The world is in the grip of the evil one, Mrs. Tazelaar. These are the last days—don't you see that?"

"I won't leave you here," Heather insisted.

"You must! You know most everything. You must find help. Do it, please, for your husband, for what they've been doing to—"

Her eyes closed. She sighed twice, then became limp.

Heather knew that she had to run, had to reenter the tunnel, had to find someone somewhere who would not cave in to the likes of Stelzfuss or the others.

She stood and headed back to the opening. She was about to enter it when she was knocked off her feet, taking the upper part of the entrance with her as dirt and roots and leaves fell around and on her.

The man she had struck!

There was a cut on the side of his face, a deep one. And he was enraged.

His hands closed around her neck.

He smelled of sweat and tobacco smoke and alcohol. His weight was at least double her own.

She started gasping for air.

Lord, I—

Suddenly the man began screaming.

120

Heather felt his hands loosen from her throat and saw him stagger back. As he turned, Heather saw that his back was *covered with black, furry tarantulas!* She saw several crawling toward her!

She ran into the tunnel, tripping over rocks and thick protruding roots, getting to her feet, running again. Finally she slowed down, the sun outside no longer penetrating the darkness in the tunnel.

She could see very little. She could smell the musty odors and hear faint sounds, movement inside the tunnel, scratching sounds, like claws across rock.

Heather stood still, the exertion of running and the impact of the sealed-in heat causing her to pant.

She realized that she had not changed her clothes in all the time that had passed since leaving her home, the blouse she wore unredeemably stained and dirty as well as torn at the shoulders; her jeans were in much the same state.

She started trembling, the total, apparently hopeless isolation and danger she faced gripping her nerves.

Lord, I go from this tunnel to where? she thought. *What do I find on the other side? What if they're waiting for me?*

And Heather didn't fully understand who *they* were . . . mere shadow figures in a nightmare that was not born out of her imagination but that came from reality itself.

After pausing several minutes, she started walking farther into the tunnel, alert for sounds behind her as well as in front.

Her clothes seemed like a new layer of skin, sticking to her body. It was hot, humid—like a tropical environment.

As such, it caused more than tarantulas to flourish. Heather saw other creatures, sometimes just their blood-red eyes almost iridescent in the darkness, often the faintest outline of

121

scampering bodies, moving quickly as she entered their world for the first time.

Things hissed at her. Other things ran over her now-bare feet.

She stepped on rocks that sent pain through her legs. Her feet touched piles of whatever-it-was that *squished* like jello underneath them.

And snakes.

Heather had seen what must have been lizards in the tunnel, but now she knew she was encountering only snakes, coiled up only a few yards away.

Rattling.

She heard the sound and moved quickly, but with no idea of whether she would encounter more in the direction in which she was heading.

And then, minutes later, she saw thin streams of daylight!

Adrenaline surged through every part of her body as that light came into the tunnel via inch-thick holes.

Holes dug by tarantulas—*a whole horde of them!*

Their shapes were apparent in the resulting illumination, on the floor of the tunnel, along the walls, hanging from roots that poked through the ceiling.

Heather had to get past the creatures in order to continue toward the other end of the tunnel.

She froze, not wanting to do what she must, the sight of her assailant being covered by them fresh in her mind.

I can't go back, she told herself. *But how can I go forward?*

She took a step to her right, then another.

A tarantula dropped down on her shoulder. It stayed there for a moment, then crawled down her arm and to the ground.

"Only the African kind are deadly. These hurt no more than a common bee sting, Mrs. Tazelaar."

Heather could feel another land on the top of her head and start to work its way through her hair.

As she brought her hand up to brush it off, she stopped suddenly.

If I don't react, if I pretend they aren't dangerous, maybe they won't attack me, she thought. *Isn't that what Ophelia meant when she told me, "Don't bother them and they won't hurt you, even a little"?*

Another step, followed by—

The tarantula had crawled down her forehead and over the bridge of her nose, pausing as two of its sticky feet entered her nostrils, probing them.

Oh God, help me!

She could feel another doing the same thing with her left ear.

Her stomach started to constrict, and she wanted to let out a very loud scream. But Heather managed to clamp her mouth shut, sensing that at least one of the tarantulas would try to enter it otherwise, out of curiosity or instinct, and that would be something she could not endure.

Then Heather turned a corner. Directly ahead she saw a welcome flood of yellow light.

14

★ ★ ★

A major highway.

Heather brushed the last spider from her hair as she walked out of the tunnel. She said a silent prayer of thanks.

The village where Ophelia and the others had been living was nestled in a mountain range that, farther north, became quite a scenic area for tourists. And the highway just in front of Heather was the main link that had been used for many years, traveled by people from most of the eastern and southern states.

They pass right by on their way to having fun, she thought, *without realizing what pain lies just a little to the east!*

A grassy slope directly ahead led down to steel guardrails on that side of the highway. The traffic was heavy at that time of the morning. People were traveling to the lush countryside up north, or returning to where they happened to live, or going to work at whatever businesses existed in that immediate area.

Heather knew she had to get someone to give

her a ride, and she wasn't concerned about where the destination was, so long as there was a phone she could use.

But who am I going to call? she asked herself. *Becky's gone . . . Nick's gone . . . his fellow agents are gone.*

She hadn't understood how few people she really knew. Becky and Nick were more completely her whole world than she had been willing to admit. It was a problem she suspected many widows had to face. Even in an age of so-called feminine liberation, old social patterns still hung on.

I don't have any bank account that I can call my own. There was no time to get one established before . . . all this happened. I signed everything as Nick's wife, but now it's all tied up in—

The attorney!

Surely he could be trusted. Nick wouldn't have hired him otherwise.

Heather regretted that she hadn't thought of Lloyd Brahill previously. Nick had hinted over the years that he was far more than he seemed, that to call him just an attorney was simplistic to the extreme.

"He has a great deal of power, this man," Nick told her at one point. "I am very glad he's on our side."

If she could find some way to reach him by phone, he might know exactly what she should do.

She saw a truck approach. Piled up in the back were two large deer. She turned her head away as she saw the look of pain and fear on their faces.

How can I expect anyone to pick me up? she admitted to herself. *Ophelia was able to get me a bath, and she cleaned my clothes as well as she could under the circumstances, but now I'm a mess.*

The truck seemed to be going on past, but then it stopped

a dozen yards or so to her right, pulling over to the shoulder of the road.

She ran up to it.

The driver had gotten out and rushed around the front.

"Are you all right?" he asked, frowning. "You look as though you've been through hell itself!"

"In some respects, mister," she replied, smiling weakly, "you're not at all far from the truth."

"What can I do to help?" he asked.

The man was just short of six feet tall, in his mid-thirties, not bad looking, with long coal-black hair.

"I need to get away from here," she said, "and I need to find a phone."

"I have a phone in the truck," he told her, "and in five minutes this place will be only a memory."

"What's your name?"

"Gary Schorp. Yours?"

"He . . . Helen Thomas."

They shook hands, and then he opened the door to the passenger's side. After she had climbed up onto the front seat, he shut the door, hurried back around the front of the truck, and jumped inside.

As Schorp settled behind the brown, leather-wrapped steering wheel, he started to stick some plugs in his ears.

"What are they for?" she asked.

"My ears are very sensitive," he told her. "This cabin isn't insulated well, not like a luxury car's. The road and wind noise are just too loud for me. I have an extra set if you would like to use them."

He pointed to the center transmission hump.

"There's the phone. Call anywhere you need to, Helen."

Heather panicked as she tried to think of Lloyd Brahill's

home number and momentarily failed. Then she remembered.

"How do I dial?" she asked. "Any special procedure?"

"Just pick up the phone, switch to send, and dial."

"Thanks."

"My pleasure."

Brahill's number rang several times. Heather was about to give up when, finally, his wife, Melody, answered.

"Melody—guess who this is?" she said, finding a way to avoid giving her real name.

"Heather—Heather Tazelaar?" the voice at the other repeated.

"That's right. Is Lloyd home?"

"No. He's assigned to a miltary base for a few weeks."

"It's urgent, Melody. Where can I reach him?"

"Actually it's top secret, so I don't know where he is exactly. I have a number to call. Do you want me to—"

"Please!"

"OK, hold on. I'll see if I can get through to him."

Nearly a minute passed.

Heather's gaze drifted through the rear window of the truck, past the hunting rifle she saw on the floor, to the deer in the back.

Their faces!

Their eyes were gone.

How could that be?

Heather could see, in that instant, no clear indication that they had been shot at all, unless the bodies happened to be turned on the side that was hit in both instances and she simply couldn't see the wounds.

She was about to turn away from the pathetic sight when

she noticed a large canister next to one of the bodies. She squinted, trying to read the lettering.

"Heather, what's wrong?" The voice interrupted her attention.

She held the receiver slightly away from her ear at Lloyd Brahill's powerful baritone.

"I need help," she said. "Something's happened."

"Does it have anything to do with the file?"

"You know about it? You have a copy of it?"

"I do."

"But how?"

"Heather, it's awkward for me to tell you this but—"

She was listening, desperately anxious not to lose contact with Brahill, but she was also seeing something else: the Army boots that Schorp was wearing.

Normal perhaps for a hunter, she tried to convince herself.

"You see, I took over this case just after Nick died," Brahill's voice continued. "I had to convince myself that he wasn't just lumping together irreconcilable so-called facts and letting his imagination somehow smooth over the implausibilities."

Heather studied the earplugs that Schorp was wearing.

I wonder if they could be designed for more than just keeping out—

"What did you find out, Lloyd?" she asked, trying not to attract Schorp's attention more than she had already.

"That everything is true. It's even worse than Nick ever imagined. I've started a process, Heather, using only people I know can be trusted. It's not too late. But it means now that I'll have to have an armed escort everywhere I go."

"Yes, if they find out about you . . . ," she started to say.

Schorp's manner had changed. He was sitting back, his

wrists on the steering wheel, trying to seem nonchalant. But his smile had faded—no, twisted—into something else.

"That's the point, Heather," Brahill continued. "You're absolutely right. It's going to be tough but we'll win out, though this is going to make Watergate, Irangate, and even the McCarthy hearings play like nursery rhymes."

"They'll get violent, Lloyd," she said as she saw Schorp dropping one hand off the wheel and reaching for something at his left side. "They're everywhere, you know—!"

Strapped to Schorp's right side was a hunting knife. In a quick movement that surprised even Heather herself, she grabbed it and pressed the blade against his Adam's apple while still holding the phone receiver.

"Heather!" Brahill yelled frantically. "What's going on?"

"I'm in a truck with one of them," she replied. "Hey, what's your license number?"

Schorp said nothing.

She pressed in with the blade, just enough to draw a little blood.

"Your people murdered my husband and murdered his best friend," she said. "That's not to mention dozens of helpless people back where you picked me up, maybe hundreds more around the country!"

"Heather, is all that true?" Brahill asked.

"It is," she replied tersely. Then she addressed Schorp. "Your death's going to be downright meaningless in comparison. I want your license number."

He recited the number.

"I'll have it traced in a few minutes," Brahill said after she had repeated it to him. "This is going to be war, you know. I see something like the Colombians have been experiencing, only much, much worse."

130

"Where should I head?" she asked.

"Any idea of your location?"

"Only vaguely. It's in the Appalachian Mountains some-where."

"Look at any road signs that come up. I'll hang on. . . ."

A minute passed.

Another.

No signs.

"Where are we?" she demanded of Schorp.

"West Virginia."

"Where in West Virginia?"

He clamped his lips shut.

"Tell me now!" she yelled.

Schorp was smiling as he looked straight ahead.

A state trooper roadblock less than half a mile directly in front of them!

She told Brahill what she saw.

"They *own* some police departments," he said, "ones that they've infiltrated with Nazi sympathizers."

"What?" Heather responded, astonished.

"True, very true. That's why there's been such a rise in beatings and such of blacks . . . nothing you do now can be considered too risky, Heather. I know that. These people desperately need to get rid of everyone who *knows*—you, me, others. I'll have protection. But you won't, at least until I can get some military help. There's a cadre of *Desert Storm* vets in that area, I think."

Schorp was slowing down. Heather dropped the receiver.

"Don't!" she told him.

"You can't kill me," he said. "You need me to drive this truck."

131

"Wrong!" she proclaimed. "I'm not the frail little thing you might think I am."

"It's all yours then!" Schorp screamed suddenly as he grabbed the door handle, opened the door, and jumped out.

As Heather scrambled behind the wheel, she saw Schorp land on the soft grassy center strip of the highway.

Her eyes jumped to the rearview mirror.

At least two state trooper cars also were behind her now!

Coming up fast!

Heather noticed that the truck had a specially reinforced bumper and decided that she could do only one thing, and it had nothing to do with giving herself over to the custody of law enforcement officers who could only have been on the payroll of Stelzfuss and others like him.

They knew she would continue to be dangerous, armed as she was with the knowledge that she had gained. There would be the pretense of capturing her, reading the rights that were hers as prescribed by the Miranda Act, and then taking her off to some unknown jail where she would mysteriously die sometime during the next few hours.

At the same time, they're going to go after you, Lloyd. You may not have much more of a chance than I do. I can't count on anyone, even the army, to help me right now! I have to be prepared to die, Lord—but only You know what is ahead. Whatever it is, I know You will be there with me, here or in—!

She pressed her foot down on the accelerator.

The truck jumped ahead. She hadn't realized how powerful it would be. The surge was so strong that she figured the engine must have been altered by the owner for maximum speed.

The men kneeling behind the cars ahead of her opened fire. The truck's windshield was blown away, but Heather crouched as the bullets hit, the glass covering her, but none getting into her eyes, mouth, or nose.

She had clamped her hands on the steering wheel, keeping it as steady as she could. Just before the reinforced bumper hit the first two cars blocking the highway, she pulled herself up again and saw half a dozen men jumping to one side or the other as she felt the impact and heard metal crumple as the truck barreled through.

A dozen yards behind those first cars were two others. The truck swept them aside just as easily.

Heather was trembling badly while she concentrated on keeping the truck under control. As she glanced over her shoulder, she saw the three cars that had been behind her turn left, cross the grassy divider, and drive in the wrong direction up the highway until the first one was parallel with the truck.

A uniformed trooper opened fire at her with a semiautomatic rifle.

Heather swerved, then speeded up. Bullets hit the side of the door and the fender, but missed the interior.

Then the three patrol cars crossed back over the divider and continued pursuing her from behind.

She saw a dirt road and turned off onto it with such abruptness that she was thrown back against the front seat.

Apparently this took the troopers by surprise, and they went right on past. But she could hear tires squealing, and she knew that they realized what was happening.

The canister! If it's what I think it is!

She stopped the truck and dashed outside to the rear compartment.

The label read: *Contents Inflammable!*

More of their chemicals!

Fortunately the black, slightly rusted container, which must have held at least fifteen gallons, was on its side, and she was able to roll it near the end of the truck. After getting the lid off, she let the contents—a thick yellowish liquid with an acrid odor—drain out onto the dirt road, the canister going, too, after it was empty. Then she climbed back behind the steering wheel, drove the truck on a bit farther, and stopped.

Heather grabbed the hunting rifle in the back and hurried into the surrounding woods. Seconds later, she heard the patrol cars.

The first one approached the puddle of chemicals and stopped inches from it.

They've seen it, she told herself. *Somehow they've seen it!*

Two troopers got out, walked over to it.

"I know exactly what it is," one of them said.

"So do I," the other agreed. "I think Schorp had the canister in the back of his truck."

"It's what killed the deer."

"And a lot else. We'll bypass it. I don't want any heat or sparks from our motors setting it off."

They went back to the two other cars and told the drivers what to do, then returned to their own.

As the first patrol car was turning slightly into the woods, Heather aimed the rifle and shot out the back right tire. The patrol car swerved, its left fender glancing off a tree, then flipped over on its side.

The second patrol car couldn't stop in time and banged into it. The third one came to a halt less than a foot from the puddle.

The first car's underside faced her, the gas tank in her clear line of fire.

Heather, drenched in perspiration, narrowed her eyes,

closed her finger around the trigger, and fired the rifle. The bullet missed. She tried once more.

The bullet hit its target.

Less than a second later, the gasoline became a mass of flame. This ignited the chemicals, which exploded with such force that the third squad car, so near the puddle, was thrown several feet into the air. It landed against a large, thick-trunked tree, bounced off it, and then what was left of it settled into the middle of the dirt road, every inch of its frame ablaze. The two other patrol cars were also engulfed.

Heather had been knocked off her feet. As she struggled to stand, she saw one of the troopers stumbling toward her, his body covered with flame. He was screaming wildly, flailing his arms through the air, until he fell down less than a dozen feet from her.

Within hours of being found, Erik Stelzfuss had been flown to Oahu, Hawaii, his private jet landing at an isolated airstrip on the windward side of the island. On board was a famed plastic surgeon, along with a leading dermatologist and other surgeons, as well as aides to the group of them.

Stelzfuss's body was covered with a special gel, and he was wrapped in a paper-thin sheet of polytetrafluoroethylene, which was molded to his body but could be easily removed without touching him. The special bandages covering his nose and mouth had been hastily constructed of the same substance in order to keep as much pressure as possible off the damaged skin of that part of his face.

He was now on a special air bed being treated with medicines to keep down infection, and his doctors were grafting onto him a new artificial skin that would coexist with his body, resisting antibiotic rejection until new human skin was generated, dissolving the man-made variety. All of this an example of what his billions could buy for him.

Three groups of specialists working in tandem!

Nearly nine-and-a-half hours later, billionaire arms merchant Erik Stelzfuss was wheeled out of the operating room of the small clinic, which overlooked the renowned North Shore surfing area of Oahu.

Sedation didn't start to wear off until noon of the next day. His enormous body was restrained by feather-light yet iron-strong straps so that he could not tear loose any of the artificial skin.

His eyelids lifted slowly, and he spoke with a harsh voice as he saw someone familiar standing over him.

"Josef . . . ," he said so weakly that the other man had to bend down close to Stelzfuss's mouth in order to hear him.

"Yes, Erik, my friend."

"Is he in the next room . . . as I asked?"

"Yes. But I don't think seeing him, even briefly, would be such a good idea right now, Mr. Stelzfuss."

"Just . . . for a moment. Do it . . . Josef!"

Nodding reluctantly, the man, himself old and bent, left that room for a few minutes and entered the one next door.

Sitting in a wheelchair was a long-familiar figure, someone now well into his seventies, with a steel plate in the back of his head and scars on his temple, cheeks, and neck.

An aide jumped to his feet.

"Sir!" he said. "What do you need?"

"Stelzfuss wants to see him, wants to be reassured again—perhaps, even in his present condition, to gloat as he always does that he was able to thwart the intentions of a traitorous few."

"But he goes through all this several times a year. How much longer will it go on?"

"It's become a tradition, for want of a better word, though I would think *obsession* is far more accurate."

"I see. . . ."

"Have you checked out every detail?"

"I have. He'll never notice. We were very fortunate, of course. Coincidences as good as this one are rare."

"You're right. But we mustn't be lax in any way. Everything must be as close to what it was as we can possibly manage, or else he will suspect—if not now, then later when all his faculties have returned and he is as alert as ever. We must be so careful—the hair color, the steel plate, all of it."

"Precisely, sir."

"Good. Let's humor the fat one yet another time."

The aide wheeled the frail, tortured body into Stelzfuss's room, who turned his head as much as the restraints would allow.

"It is good . . . to see you again," he said. "But as you can tell . . . I am not in good shape myself now."

There was no flicker of emotion or recognition from the battered face he spoke to.

"I wonder . . . if you have missed me," Stelzfuss added. "It . . . would give me encouragement if that were so."

Groans came from the still form in the wheelchair, groans that sounded vaguely like the beginnings of speech, but which were incoherent at best.

"Is he . . . hurting?" Stelzfuss asked with a compassion to which he was not frequently given.

"I doubt it, sir," the one named Josef replied quickly. "It might be that he is overcome with emotion at the sight of you. It has been a longer-than-usual absence, you know."

Stelzfuss started coughing, an especially painful process for him under the present circumstances.

"Josef . . . ," he said, "take him back. This was . . . a bad idea."

When he was again alone, Erik Stelzfuss realized then more than ever that he had to recover as quickly and fully as possible. There was no way he could allow that Tazelaar woman to get away with what she had done to him . . . with how she had made him look before a president of the United States.

15

★ ★ ★

Heather sat behind the steering wheel of the appropriated truck.

Behind her, three squad cars no longer belched flame, only vagrant traces of smoke now emanating from their twisted, scorched, black remains.

Her hands were shaking.

She tried to control them but failed, realizing in that moment how much she had always needed Nick throughout their years of married life.

If you and I became as one when we were married, my love, she thought, *then I am only half of what I was, so incomplete that I cannot stop aching for you, Nick. I truly must stop, I know that, but you weren't an ordinary man, and you didn't die in an ordinary way—nor is this grief I feel ordinary either.* She couldn't help feeling a thin strand of bitterness.

If you had told me, Nick, I could have been prepared somehow, perhaps taken precautions. But you were so interested in keeping me out of it, for my own protection, that you managed to drag me right into the center of everything, without a clue as to what will happen next.

Heather banged her fists against the steering wheel.

"I love you so much," she screamed. "If only I can stop hating what you've caused in my life!"

And yet she knew, as she sank back against the front seat, that Nick hadn't *caused* anything. He had been interested only in keeping her ignorant of any and all details, figuring that literally what she didn't know wouldn't hurt her. It was an accident that she had stumbled onto that file.

She closed her eyes and tried to calm herself as much as the present circumstances would permit. If she didn't take the next several hours and use them wisely, she might end up joining Nick sooner than she could have guessed.

For a moment, she wondered if that would be such a bad idea after all.

Suddenly, she heard the sounds of people running.

Her eyes shot open and her right hand instinctively went for the key in the truck's ignition.

"There's a cadre of Desert Storm vets in that area, I think."

Heather remembered what Lloyd Brahill had told her.

Within the minute, Heather was surrounded by tough-looking soldiers in combat outfits.

Lloyd Brahill himself—tall, broad-shouldered, the look of an Olympic athlete about him—had stepped out of a military vehicle directly behind the truck.

A contingent of soldiers was left behind to clean up the wreck site and to discover whatever they could about Heather's pursuers.

"You're finally safe," Lloyd Brahill told her after they had switched to an awaiting sedan he had commissioned.

"I never realized how well connected you are," she admitted. "I'm sure that's why Nick liked you so much."

"You'd be amazed, Heather, at how God has blessed me with relationships that are increasingly important, judging by what lies ahead of us."

"Right through to the president?" she asked.

"Exactly right," Brahill acknowledged. "That's where we're heading.. Lady, you've been the hottest news around!"

"The media have picked up on this?"

"With a vengeance. It may be the arms dealers' Achilles' heel."

"I thought they had enough of the media in this country sewed up so that they didn't have to worry."

"They own some cable companies, TV and radio stations, and newspapers, yes. But however influential these are, the vast majority as yet are very much beyond any kind of control on their part and still maverick enough to break this open. It's probably the biggest story of the last three decades."

"All because of me?" she asked disbelievingly.

"Not just you, Heather. It goes far deeper than that, of course, but the fact is, you are fast becoming the rallying point for everyone who wants to get the cancer represented by these characters out of politics, out of the military, out of business, and wherever else they've spread."

"But how can that be done? They're so well entrenched."

"Their group really doesn't control everything and everyone, frankly. Yet what they *do* control represents a frightening percentage, no doubt about that. The rest of us will be compelled to rise up against them—now that things are coming out in the open after so long—and perform the drastic surgery that is needed, whatever the cost."

"It's a shame that my Nick couldn't be right here in the middle of this with us, pitching and—"

Brahill placed a finger gently on her lips.

He started to say something, but was interrupted by a transmission over the specially equipped sedan's shortwave radio.

Their driver, a young private named Aaron Lotridge, accepted the connection and turned up the volume so that they could hear what was being transmitted.

"Two Apache attack helicopters behind you! Coming on fast. Head for any kind of cover you can find."

Lotridge turned his head and asked, "Sir, what do you want me to do?"

"Apaches!" Heather exclaimed before Brahill was able to answer. "How could they have gotten hold of even one of those, Lloyd?"

"I wonder about that myself."

Brahill leaned forward and asked the driver, "Do we have any *real* firepower other than what I'm able to see right now?"

A canvas-covered military transport truck carrying a dozen soldiers was just ahead of them on the highway. Behind the sedan was a modified jeep with a single high-powered machine gun and three more men.

"Not what we need against *them*," the younger man replied. "A Tomahawk missile would be great just now, but that machine gun on the jeep in back of us and the rifles the men ahead of us have—well, that's it, sir."

His forehead covered with perspiration, Lotridge fought a twitch in his right cheek, blushing as it got worse.

"Nothing we could reasonably throw against those Apaches would do the job," he said nervously. "Sir, we can only hope to outmaneuver anything that attacks us until the base sends help."

"Any Apaches there?"

"One, as far as I know, and dozens of F-16s."

"Contact the base commander immediately."

"Will do, sir. One problem though."

"What's that?"

"There's a town between us and the—"

His words were cut short as machine-gun bursts ripped through the air, missing the car and hitting the transport truck instead. Three soldiers were flung from the back, dead before they hit the asphalt. When the driver slammed on his brakes, the truck swerved into the grassy divider and the left lane of traffic coming the other way. Several cars piled into it, and the whole crumpled mass exploded with flame.

"Into the woods!" Brahill yelled.

Lotridge obeyed immediately, jumping the sedan over the highway's right shoulder and down a small embankment. It entered the woods.

"This isn't a reinforced vehicle," Lotridge pointed out. "It's going to be junk in no time, sir."

"Then we'll switch to the jeep!" Brahill barked, "after the guys catch up with us."

The sedan crashed through small young trees, then plowed head-on into a large boulder that was partially covered by moss. The front crumpled on impact, and hot steam shot out from the radiator.

The three of them were shaken badly, but were able to get out of the car. They ran for only seconds before more shots were fired from one of the Apaches. Lotridge was hit in the chest.

"The jeep!" Brahill said. "Where's the—?"

An answer came in the next instant.

The jeep came toward them, moving strictly by forward momentum. There was no driver. They could see that there was only one man left in the back of the jeep. He had been thrown forward and was slumped partway over the front seat.

"Those devils have done it!" Brahill said, astonished. "It's been cut down to just the three of us!"

"I'm not going to last very long, sir," Lotridge told him. "Leave me behind. If they start to follow you on foot, I might be able to hold them off before . . . before—"

"I will not," Brahill insisted.

The three of them made it as far as they could into the forest. Finally, Brahill could not carry Lotridge any longer. He managed to find a clear section of ground on which to rest Lotridge's body, whose shirt had turned dark with blood. He was starting to cough badly.

Lotridge reached up with his left hand and grabbed Brahill's shoulder.

"Jesus is real," he said, not above a whisper.

He sighed once, and his eyes turned up in their sockets.

Brahill turned to Heather, his eyes searching her own. "I don't know if I can do this," he said. "I'm a lawyer. I'm used to walking into a different kind of jungle. All this is new territory to me."

Heather reached out and closed Lotridge's eyelids.

"I can be with a stranger when he dies," she said, "but not my husband."

Tears began to flow.

"I buried Nick only last week. He died just a few days before that. A month ago he was still alive. I was looking forward to putting my arms around him and—"

They both had been sitting on the ground, next to Lotridge's body. Heather fell forward against Brahill's chest, her head on his shoulder. He could feel the sobs beginning deep within her, and finally, beyond any further control, she gave in to them.

He held her as gently as he could.

"We must leave now," he said after a minute. "They may be sending in men to hunt us on the ground."

"But where do we go, Lloyd?" Heather said, her voice strained. "They had *Apache* helicopters. Did they steal them?"

"Unlikely," he admitted.

"Then they must have gotten clearance. Lloyd, how could that be? How could they walk right into a military base and take the most advanced helicopters in the world *to attack us on a major highway.* This is America, *not Iraq!*"

"I don't know, Heather. These guys are well placed. But they're going to have to pay a price, I can tell you that."

She pulled away from him, her cheeks wet.

"What do you mean?" she asked.

"Their biggest advantage is that, until now, they've been able to operate in a completely clandestine manner. Stealth has kept them hidden from general exposure in the societies in which they have been making their deals."

"And all of that is out the window now!"

"Exactly, Heather. What we've just been through wasn't carefully calculated on their part. It's an act of desperation. They so hate you, they so want to annihilate you that they're like men gone insane, nothing else mattering. It may be that some of their former media lackeys are planning to assert themselves and make something really big out of what is happening."

"How could it be otherwise, Lloyd? A downed jetliner, probably part of a housing development destroyed by the rubble it generated! What more needs to happen for this to be really big?"

He rubbed his chin with his left hand.

"Unless . . ."

"What is it, Lloyd?"

"Unless these guys—and no one can call them stupid—unless they've figured out a way to blame this on some terrorist group. They could engage in whatever destruction they wanted while placing the blame on others. Such a scapegoat would divert attention from what is going out about their own activities."

"And that would mean a certain U.S. military strike against whatever country is responsible," Heather said, the idea chilling her. "A lot can be overlooked or soft-pedaled for the sake of international diplomacy. So many things have been swept under the rug in order to appease the bureaucrats in the State Department, but surely not what has just happened. And military action means possible warfare, which in turn means—"

Brahill saw that all color had drained from her face.

"You've hit a bull's-eye, Heather. More war means more weapons means more profits that they can make from both sides," Brahill added. "It goes on and on, one militaristic binge after another."

"They can't lose," she remarked. "They do whatever it is that they want, blame some group of terrorists, stir up trouble, and pocket more profits because the international arms market has been shaken up."

Sounds.

Both stopped talking.

A deer dashed in front of them and disappeared into the surrounding forest.

Brahill breathed an exaggerated sigh of relief.

"I'm going to get the machine gun from the jeep," he said.

"It's removable, portable?" Heather asked, surprised.

146

"After a fashion. . . ."

"You know a lot about these things."

"I have plenty of military-type clients," Brahill told her. "Make sure you grab Lotridge's pistol, just in case."

He left, and she waited. As she was reaching for the pistol, Heather noticed that Lotridge's wallet had fallen out of his pocket. She picked it up, opened it, saw snapshots of his wife, two sons, and a daughter.

And now he's dead, too, she thought. *What are those four human beings going to do without him? Praise God that Nick and I never had any children to suffer through this nightmare. . . .*

Children.

How much they had wanted at least one child. As each year of married life passed with still no pregnancy, they became periodically depressed, half-questioning a God who would deny the two of them the realization of such a sweet and normal and God-ordained desire as raising a family.

Finally the two of them gave up hoping at all, gave up praying for a baby from natural childbirth. Not long before Nick disappeared, they had begun discussing the possibility of adopting a child.

Screams.

Lloyd Brahill's voice.

"Heather, run!" she could hear him shout.

This was followed by the sound of machine-gun fire.

She jumped to her feet, turned to run, then saw Brahill stumble into the little clearing. He was still holding the large gun—but just barely.

"You must go!" he demanded. "Now, Heather!"

Just then, breaking through the surrounding trees, she saw

half a dozen men dressed in black leather jackets and slacks. Each was armed with a semiautomatic rifle.

Brahill opened fire on them before they had a chance to react.

Heather ran, branches snapping across her face, stinging her. Minutes passed, her heart pounding, fast, loud.

Sounds of struggle behind her died away for the moment.

But she could not stop. She had to keep running.

The wooded area started to thin out a short distance ahead of her. And, a bit farther on, Heather came to what made her start laughing with utter, intoxicating relief.

A large expanse of asphalt, and in the middle, a medium-sized shopping mall.

It had two levels and didn't seem particularly large or elaborate, the siding not of brick or imported stone, but plain stucco that had been painted a light tan color.

They'll stop at the edge, where I am now, and not go ahead after me, Heather told herself. *Too many witnesses. That wouldn't be their style.*

She walked forward, her chest pounding, as she anticipated alerting someone and getting help.

The parking lot was virtually full, with only an occasional space empty. A few people were getting out of their cars, and they looked at her curiously, some hesitating until Heather had passed by. She could see that a number of others were pointing at her and whispering among themselves.

It's the way I look! she exclaimed to herself. *They're probably wondering what jail or sanitarium I escaped from!*

Other shoppers were leaving the mall and stopped as she approached, their expressions fearful.

One of the entrances was only a hundred feet or so ahead.

She saw a middle-aged security guard, tall, with strong-looking shoulders, and a stomach that undoubtedly he wished he didn't have. He came through the door, sauntered on up to her, a look of disdain on his weathered face.

"Ma'am, where are you going?" he asked.

"Inside," she said as calmly as her taut nerves would allow. "I need help."

"I imagine you do," he replied, a smirk edging up the sides of his mouth.

"We shouldn't be wasting time, sir. There's no telling what they might do."

"They, ma'am? And who would *they* be?"

"They destroyed a military transport truck back on the highway near here, and all of the soldiers in it. Then they—"

The guard's manner changed.

"When was that?" he asked.

"Maybe an hour ago, or longer. It's hard for me to tell. They've been chasing me ever since and—"

His eyes widened as he glanced over her shoulder.

"Run!" he yelled.

"Now?" she asked, alarmed.

"Now!"

Heather looked in the same direction the guard had been gazing, and saw black-leather-clad figures emerging from the wooded area that had thinned out by the time it reached the parking lot.

They were heading straight for her.

She started to run.

Shots.

Car windows shattered. People began to scream. The guard had crouched down on his knees. He stood for an instant, fired his sidearm twice, and managed to hit one of the intruders.

"Hurry!" he yelled as he glanced over at her.

149

She ran in a bent-over position past three rows of cars and made it to the entrance just as bullets missed her, shattering the sliding glass doors instead.

Startled shoppers inside the mall jumped aside as she jumped through the now-bare doorframes.

"Where's the manager's office?" Heather asked a scared mother with a little girl holding tight to her hand.

The woman tried to get past her.

"Do you know?" Heather begged.

"Get away from here," the woman yelled. *"Leave us alone!"*

A young man dressed in cutaway jeans and a muscle shirt that showed off his build rushed over to them.

"Didn't you hear her?" he demanded.

"Yes!" Heather told him. "But don't you know what's going on outside? Look at what they did to the entrance."

"The door broke, that's all."

Heather pushed past him and rushed farther into the mall.

Shoppers stepped out of her way as they tried to decide whether she was just a garden variety kook to be pitied or someone quite dangerous who should be confined as soon as possible.

Heather rushed past a stationary store, a bakery, a clothing outlet, a children's toy store, a couple of fast food restaurants, a paint store, and various others.

"I need to find the security office," she kept saying. "Please, help me find the security office."

No one listened.

Communities in that area tended to be insular, not trusting strangers, and there she was, not only a stranger but a disheveled, dirt-smudged one in torn clothes mumbling something that few of them could understand.

Heather could not go on any longer. She found a plain

wood bench and sat down, her lungs gasping for air, her nerves raw.

A moment later, she felt a gentle hand on her left shoulder. She looked up.

It was a woman about her age, but taller, having a more weathered-looking face with deep lines across the forehead and turquoise-blue eyes. She was dressed in a plain white blouse and medium-brown skirt, her long red hair sparkling from the overhead lights in the mall.

"I'm Estelle Breuer," she said. "I manage this mall. I understand that you've been having a bad time."

Estelle! In a shopping mall!

Heather kept quiet. She wanted to make sure this was the same Estelle she was supposed to find.

"Your security guard," she said instead. "I know that man can help. He saw part of what was happening."

"I'm sure he can," Estelle assured her. "Will you follow me?"

The woman pulled Heather into a little "alley" between two stores. At the end was a door with an exit sign above it.

"He *did* tell me everything," she said sharply. "He's waiting in my office. I want to handle this in as discreet a manner as possible, believe that, whoever you are. If your frantic behavior continues, if *I* begin to show any emotion whatever to those people out there, we will have a king-sized panic in this building, just as surely as if someone yelled fire!

"They don't know what to expect from you since you're a stranger to this area and might be capable of anything. Me, they know where I'm coming from. Can you understand what I'm telling you?"

Heather hesitated, studying her, not knowing how to react.

"We don't have much time, I'm afraid," Estelle said, a nervous, impatient edge in her voice.

"What are you saying?"

"I am saying that all telephone communications have been cut off. Even the pay phones. Whoever is responsible got to the control boxes and disabled them."

"Why don't you send someone—?"

"Enough!" Estelle said, in a low but firm whisper. "We'll talk more when I get to my office. *Understood?*"

Heather nodded, now convinced that she was being told the truth.

16

★ ★ ★

The guard's name was Robert Gridley.

"When Heather here ran," he observed, after names were exchanged, as he sat in a rusting metal folding chair next to the manager's old, battered desk, "and I'd shot one of those guys, the rest of 'em started to move onto the parking lot with a frenzy. Man, I got to tell you that I knew right away they was after me, for revenge, and as strange as they looked, I got chills all over my body!"

He cleared his throat, trying to keep his emotions in check. "Well, a couple of hunters who were finished shopping saw what was happening and, bless them both, grabbed rifles from their trucks and started firing at those characters, too. In just a little while, the ones that were left had to retreat back into the woods. This was when our guys held up their weapons and whooped and hollered, and I gotta admit, it was a proud moment—a *real* proud moment!"

"Where are they now?" Heather asked.

"I told them to wait for the cops."

"The one call I managed to get out," Estelle interjected.

"But that won't be enough!" Heather told him. "You don't understand who these people are."

"Some terrorists, that's what," Gridley responded. "We aren't afraid of their kind out here. We've been taking care of ourselves for a long time. We're proud of the way we've been able to exist in this area, away from the big cities in a pocket of the world that's all our own. We're like those Mennonites or those Amish people. We have what we need right here."

"I can accept what you say, and I'm real happy for you, but this time your police won't be able to stand up against the firepower that these guys have."

"Some hunters and I have done that already, ma'am."

"But they have helicopters and—"

Gridley sucked in his breath.

"I was afraid of that," he admitted. "So all of this is connected then, that business on the highway a couple of hours ago and your . . . your problem?"

"It is," Heather assured him.

"And word has now spread throughout this place," Estelle said somberly. "Small towns spread news like wildfire."

Behind her desk was a window that overlooked the mall. People were obviously reacting in fear to what they had found out.

"The hunters, I betcha," Gridley said. "Real macho types, you know. They just can't keep their mouths shut about something like this. They've probably been braggin', especially to the womenfolk."

"It's not only that," Estelle added. "How do you explain a shattered front entrance, bullet hole–covered cars in the parking lot, and the bodies of some strangers wearing black leather

154

outfits? And I'm sure the fact that the pay phones are not operational has hardly helped the situation."

She stood, then walked around the big old desk. "I think they should be told the the truth, but as little of it as possible."

Heather and Gridley followed her out of the office.

Directly outside was a control panel for the mall's loudspeaker system, and a microphone was attached to it.

Estelle activated it, then held the microphone a few inches from her mouth, hesitating as she thought of what to say.

"This is the manager," she spoke, as emotionlessly as she could manage. "You are all aware by now that we have had a real unusual situation here. To get to the point, as screwy as it sounds, someone from Washington, D.C., was kidnaped a few hours ago but managed to escape. She found herself just outside this mall. Those who had held her captive were in pursuit. Our guard Robert Gridley and some of you menfolk returned their fire and made those guys flee!"

Most of the men, women, and children on the two floors let out with loud, collective cheers.

"In a short while, we will be joined by Sheriff Amos Evans and his deputies," Estelle continued. "Believe me, everything seems to be under control. An investigation is going to be launched with the help of the federal authorities. Now please, relax, all of you. Everything will be fine."

She turned off the speaker system.

"I hope that does it," she told Heather and Gridley. "I'm told I have a commanding presence. When I was put in this job, apparently that was a big point in my favor."

"I wonder . . . ," Heather mused.

"About my presence?"

"No, about whether everything is under control."

155

"Why wouldn't it be?" Estelle asked with an apprehensive tone, as the three of them reentered her office.

"Too much is at stake."

Estelle slammed the door behind her.

"There's *more*, isn't there? You've dropped just the first shoe. What's the other one all about?"

Heather struggled with how much else to to tell them.

According to the file Nick had hidden, as well as what Lloyd Brahill and others had been saying, the international arms cartel epitomized by Erik Stelzfuss had undercover agents everywhere. But did that include an isolated shopping mall in a state as small and as poor as West Virginia? Then again, it wasn't much of a mall in the first place—it needed repair and looked long overdue for some fresh paint. But it was all the people could afford and all that the merchandise suppliers would risk.

"Have you heard of the Tuskegee Project?" she asked.

Color drained instantly from Estelle Breuer's face.

"You have . . . haven't you?" Heather said as she noticed this.

"Yes . . . ," the other woman began. "I've heard of that monstrous—"

Her hands were shaking.

Gridley hurried to Estelle's side and took her hands gently in his own until she had steadied herself.

"We all have been privy to bits and pieces about it," he said after he had sat down again. "You know, ma'am, every one of us has friends who are stuck there."

"Black friends?" Heather asked foolishly.

"Yes, *black* friends," he shot back. "Not everybody hates 'em in these parts, you know. Ain't that somethin'."

"Sorry . . . ," she said, blushing.

"It's all right," Gridley replied sympathetically. "After what you've been through, well, it's all right, ma'am."

He turned to Estelle.

"For her, it's worse, though," he said, "I gotta say that, much worse."

She waved her hand through the air.

"Let me be the one to tell her, Robert," she insisted. "I feel better now, for the time being, anyway."

She swallowed hard a couple of times, then looked at Heather.

"You were there, weren't you?" Heather asked. "Where they've been kept? You're the one those two intelligence agents told me I'd be meeting."

"And *you're* the widow they mentioned to me?" Estelle replied, her eyes widening in recognition.

Heather nodded.

"Did you meet Ophelia?" Estelle asked.

"I did."

"She's my grandmother."

Heather looked at Estelle in shock.

"That surprises you, doesn't it?" Estelle observed, perversely enjoying the moment. "I don't look like what they used to call a mulatto, do I?"

Heather had to agree that she didn't.

"But how was it that Ophelia ended up in the Tuskegee Project?"

"This monstrous character married my mother, she became pregnant, and then he had both my mother and Ophelia judged insane. After being appointed their legal guardian, he signed them both away to Tuskegee."

"But why?"

157

"They needed two more guinea pigs. Mengele and the others—"

"Josef Mengele *is* alive then!" exclaimed Heather.

"Living in Hawaii where my father has been surrounding him with all the protection that money can buy. Anyway, Tuskegee was two *volunteers* short. My father wasn't opposed to getting them any way he could."

"He really does sound like a monster."

"He is . . . all 435 pounds of him!"

For a few seconds, that didn't register with Heather.

. . . all 435 pounds of him!

As soon as it did, she moved uncomfortably around in the chair.

"What's wrong?" Estelle asked. "You act as though you've met my father."

"In a way, I have," Heather replied.

"Explain."

"He's the man behind my husband's murder, I think."

"My father?" It was Estelle's turn to be nonplussed. "You've *got* to tell me more than what you have," she said plaintively.

Heather gave her other details of what had been happening over the past few weeks, from the day she was informed of Nick's death to what she saw of a very large man running into the woods, much of his body aflame.

"I hope he burnt all the way down to ashes," Estelle reacted.

"I've got to ask why you haven't gotten the federal government involved," Heather said.

"It's not that I haven't tried, but there've been only dead ends. It all boils down to what they call proof. And they don't count a bunch of dying blacks as proof of anything. There was

158

one CIA agent who seemed our best hope, but like everyone else, he left, and we never heard anything further."

Heather almost didn't want to ask the question that came to mind then.

"Can you tell me what his name was?" she said finally, dreading what she might hear.

"Nick, I'm sure that that's what it was . . . Nick-something . . . I just can't remember his last name right now."

She saw tears well up in Heather's eyes.

"What is it?" she said softly. "What's wrong, honey?"

"He was my husband."

Estelle slumped back in her chair.

"I'm real sorry," she said. "I had no way of knowing."

"He's dead. That's why he never got back to you. His body was found in a ditch outside Düsseldorf, Germany."

"What a nightmare you've had," Estelle said with a groan and tears in her eyes as well. "First, you lose somebody you love, then you have to run for your life. And then we all here jump on you like *you're* the criminal."

Both were silent for several minutes. Gridley waited patiently, sensitive enough to leave them with their thoughts and not interrupt.

"What a crazy, rotten mess for both of us!" Estelle said. "My father promised my mother everything if she would marry him. She was so beautiful that if she hadn't been desperate, she would never have considered such a pig as that man. But she was so poor, so very poor, my dear, dear mother. Ophelia and she were close to starvation."

"But you don't seem to have suffered any of the consequences of the experimentation that the others suffered." Heather spoke slowly, still recovering from a fresh surge of

159

memories with Nick at the center. "You have a good job, better than most in this area, I imagine."

"Oh, but what you see isn't what you get. People seem to admire my hair. But they don't realize that there's nothing underneath. It's all false, the best wig I could buy, with what little money I could scrape together."

"Anything else?"

"Oh yes. I can never have children of my own. I'm completely sterile."

Heather was silent for a moment.

"Estelle?" she asked.

"Yes?"

"I could never have children either. Nick and I were thinking about adopting at least one child just before . . . before they killed him."

"Your Nick must have been a wonderful man."

"You're not married?"

"No. It's not only that I'm sterile, Heather. It's more. My plumbing's been messed around with, before I was ever born. I'm all messed up, and in ways that I can never talk about to anyone. Sure, you don't see what's wrong on the outside. But I probably won't live to be forty. I get severe headaches several times a week.

"I see women who have a child, maybe two or three. Their marriages are solid. They're happy being wives and mothers. They come to the mall all the time with their little ones hanging onto their hands or being carried in their arms. Or they're pregnant. And I wonder if I want to live at all. They just remind me of what I can never have."

She leaned forward on the desk.

"But you know what was the worst for me?" she asked.

Heather shook her head.

"The fact that Erik Stelzfuss had been going unpunished. I know all about forgiveness. But I don't think I can ever come that far—in the same way, I suppose, that God is unlikely ever to forgive Satan."

"Because Satan would never ask."

"You got that right! If my father ever asked me to forgive him, I . . . I don't know what I would do. How can so much agony be overlooked?"

Heather didn't pursue the matter any further, and she changed the subject.

"Shouldn't we be downstairs now, waiting for the police to come?" she suggested, though not able to conceal her skepticism about their capabilities.

"You don't think they have a chance, do you?" Estelle asked.

"If the men who answer to Stelzfuss and others of his ilk are determined to get to me, only an army is going to be able to stop them."

"We have a military base near here."

"I know, but we're not able to call anybody there. Even if we did, what would we say? That terrorists of some kind are probably going to attack sometime soon? Would they believe us? Or would they think it was some sort of crank call?"

"I really don't think there's going to be a problem," Estelle added. "I mean, how do they know someone wasn't able to contact the base?"

"They don't. But they take risks, these people. Every time they sell guns, risk is involved. That doesn't bother them at all."

"If it gets really bad, one of the cops can radio on through to the base. Any kind of call like *that* should be taken very seriously, don't you think?"

"I have to agree, but by then it might be too late."

"We'll just have to see," Estelle said as she stood and headed for the door. "It's not that we have a lot of options just now."

"We have one other," Gridley commented.

"What's that?" Heather asked.

"I could drive to the base."

"That would take an hour," Estelle reminded the man. "And any of us could do that."

"But you're the one who said that we don't have much in the way of choices. Look, you can have the sheriff send a message if everything's all right. If there's nothing after I get to the base, I'll know that you'll need at least some of that army Heather here was mentioning."

Estelle was smiling as she replied, "For a lifelong hick, you've got something going upstairs there!"

Gridley reached out, hugged her, then hurried from the office, down the escalator nearby, and outside to the parking lot, where he jumped into his battered truck and took off as fast as the old vehicle would allow him.

"I hope you're wrong," Estelle remarked. "I like that man. He's big and kind of stupid looking, but he's honest, with a wife and three children. I'd hate to see him brought back in a body bag."

"You're starting to believe I might be right then?"

"You could be dead wrong, Heather, for all I know. But I don't fancy myself as suicidal. What happens here is a big responsibility of mine."

She unlocked the center drawer of her desk and withdrew a large manila envelope, then hugged it to her chest for a moment.

"I have lived less than forty years," she said, her voice

cracking, "but there has been so much that has happened. I wonder sometimes when there will be anything but pain of one sort or another."

She handed the envelope to Heather.

"This is something I showed to your husband," she said.

"Are you sure you want me to see it?" Heather asked.

Estelle nodded.

The envelope seemed well packed, heavy. Heather carefully emptied the contents onto her lap and saw that there were mostly photographs inside, together with a few handwritten letters.

A man in a wheelchair, his back to the camera.

"Stelzfuss handed that over to my mother," Estelle recalled. "He seemed eager for her to see it, she told me. Look at the snapshots around the fringes of the picture, on the table next to the wheelchair, and the wall on either side."

The man was facing double sliding-glass doors. On the wall to the left were many photos, some framed, some just stuck there, presumably with tacks or tape. It was the same to the right of where he was sitting.

"Can you make out any of the shots?" Estelle asked.

"Not really."

"I had a friend from the local police department magnify some of them for me."

"What did you find?"

"This is going to sound heavy-duty strange. And that's a promise."

"Go on. Nothing will seem odd to me from now on."

"The ones I studied were all of—" she swung her chair around and faced Heather directly— "members of the Kennedy family."

Heather agreed that that was peculiar but added, "Lots of people are fixated on the Kennedys."

"That's what I thought," Estelle agreed, "until my cop friend accidentally magnified the back of that man's head."

"The one in the wheelchair?"

"You got it, Heather. Do you have any idea what showed up?"

"None."

"A rectangular-shaped bump and a scar clear around it."

"He has a metal plate there?"

"Right again. Just like John Fitzgerald Kennedy might have had if, somehow, he'd survived the assassination attempt!"

This startled Heather. Everything on her lap scattered on the floor.

"Sorry . . . ," she said as she bent over to pick it all up.

"Can't blame you," Estelle added. "I went kind of crazy for awhile afterward because another of those photos shows my father standing next to the man in the wheelchair!"

Heather came upon the one she had mentioned. There was no denying Erik Stelzfuss's bulk.

"He has his hand on the other man's shoulder. And he's smiling."

"Do we *really* have any idea what this is all about?" Estelle mused. "I mean, there were stories at the time that the coffin was switched before anything was loaded onto Air Force One. Remember that?"

"I do. But JFK would be in his seventies by now," Heather pointed out.

"Look at what we can *see*, Heather. That man has white hair. The backs of his hands are terribly wrinkled. And he's not sitting up straight in the wheelchair but is bent over a bit, just like an elderly person would be."

"Why would Stelzfuss allow such a revealing picture ever to get out of his possession? You'd think that that would be the last thing he'd want to happen!"

"Yes, but remember, mother was still not more than a plain-and-simple black to this man. Beautiful, yes, but a black just the same. And there's no telling when it was—"

Heather did a little speculation of her own. "How she got it, I couldn't guess, but she probably felt she needed it as an ace up her sleeve. If your father ever tried to get out of his promises to her, then she would force him into keeping them. I wonder sometimes if putting someone like you in charge of a mall like this was a long-term part of the deal."

Estelle said nothing at first. "I don't know why, but that never occurred to me," she finally replied. "I tend to get lost in the details of the photo itself and not think of how it is that I actually have it here now."

Heather glanced through the rest of the contents, then returned them to the envelope and handed it over to Estelle.

"You know what?" Estelle said, trying to be cheerful. "We've got to get you some new clothes. This mall has a factory outlet store for one of the leading dress manufacturers. Bless them, I did what I could to convince them that they should jump in, and they did, modestly, but they *are* here. It's not what you're used to, but at least the clothes are clean."

"But I have no way to pay for them," Heather reminded her, "at least not until I get back home."

"You'll be my guest. The mall will pick up the bill for whatever you need, my friend."

"Best offer I've had in a long time, Estelle."

"Good!"

165

Heather had to admit that she felt better after getting into some new clothes. A new floral-patterned blouse and a pair of jeans made all the difference, along with the fact that it seemed the people pursuing her actually had given up.

She was growing to like Estelle Breuer very much. Estelle reminded Heather of Becky Huizinga. Hardly a minute passed when Heather didn't wonder—and worry—about her best friend's fate.

The crowd was becoming understandably impatient.

"Nobody's going to hurt us now," a plump woman in her mid-thirties said irritably as Estelle and Heather approached. "We're beginning to feel like prisoners now. I thought the danger had passed."

"That seems to be the case," Estelle replied. "But I don't think we should take any chances."

"We can wait," somebody else shouted her down. "Lady, keep quiet, will ya?"

A short while later, the first of three local patrol cars pulled up in front of the main entrance.

"The sheriff's here," a teenaged girl said excitedly. "That's great!"

Amos Evans must have been six-feet-eight-inches tall.

"How in the world does he manage to fit into that car?" Heather asked.

"Amos had to have the seat especially built, as well as lower the floor on the driver's side," Estelle told her. "And he drives with the seat tilted back quite a bit."

As he and his deputies walked toward the entrance, there was a sudden gust of air, blowing their hats off their heads, followed by a loud whirling noise.

"*No!*" Heather screamed.

The two Apache attack copters were back, rising up over the tops of the woods nearby and swooping in like birds of prey on a herd of helpless sheep!

In an instant the three squad cars had been reduced to flaming piles of metal. Only Evans made it alive as he ran past the open doorframe, screaming when his jacket started to catch fire.

17

★ ★ ★

The helicopters had disappeared from view.

"They just wanted to assert themselves, to show who was in control," Sheriff Evans said as he put on a clean shirt from another department of the same store where Heather had gotten her own new clothes.

The back of his neck was sore, and he had some singed hair ends, but several people in the crowd had acted immediately, saving him from any greater harm by putting out the fire almost as soon as it had started.

"We're used to fires around here," he said as he emerged from the changing room wearing a bright yellow shirt. "The dry season each year means danger day in and day out. Our folk have been well trained over the years."

"You must know about the Tuskegee Project, Sheriff," Heather remarked bluntly. "You don't seem like a man who can be easily intimidated. Why haven't you done anything about those poor people?"

"There was sure a time when I wouldn't have agreed with you, ma'am," Evans replied honestly.

"About what? You've lost me."

"About calling them people, that's what I mean. Coons maybe, darkies, niggers—that's what I would have named them, but not people. Many of us thought of them as dogs to be trained to serve us, and that's that."

He noticed the expression on Heather's face.

"You've been raised as a Yankee all your life," he said, though not in a gruff manner. "That's all you know, the Northern way of thinking, and I can't fault you for that. But for me, for Estelle here, for most everybody out there in the mall, it's been just the opposite from the word go. The lot of us have been steeped in the ways of the South all our lives. It's hard for anybody to break away."

"But you sound as though you've started to do just that."

"I have. . . ."

"What caused the change?"

"Something sudden."

"What was that?"

Evans looked around the clothing store, trying to avoid eye contact.

"Seeing it all back there," he continued.

"In that village, with the Tuskegee victims?"

"Yeh. That. Knowing Estelle. Learning what awful things happened to her beautiful mother."

His voice dropped to nearly a whisper.

"Seeing the blind, the lame, the disfigured, the retarded . . . so hopeless . . . nobody doing a thing for them . . . everyone turning their backs and walking away, with them people's cries in the background."

Heather saw tears trickling down the weathered face.

170

"They were no animals," he went on, "though they were sure as hell being treated that way."

"If there are any animals in this, it's the men who experimented on them," Heather offered.

Evans spun around on his heels.

"How right you are!" he said, his voice rising. "They must be monsters in human flesh, so normal looking on the outside but . . . but . . ."

His face was becoming quite red.

"I started digging," he told her, "putting together bits and pieces. I was working pretty closely with someone from the CIA itself."

Heather walked up to Evans.

"Was his name Nick?" she asked.

"Yeh, that's it."

"My husband. Nick was my husband."

Evans glanced at Estelle who was nodding.

"Was?" he repeated.

"His body was found in Germany . . . outside Düsseldorf."

Evans sat down in a nearby folding chair, burying his large head in his hands.

"He was so honest, so decent," he said. "I was planning to take some vacation time and head on up—"

He jumped to his feet, rage building.

"I'm going to hang these devils," he bellowed. "I have photos. I know this area so well. I hid where they couldn't have suspected and snapped hundreds of shots. I processed every roll myself!"

"Shots of what?" Heather asked.

"Not *what,* ma'am. People. Government types in some cases."

Heather's palms started to sweat.

171

"What do you mean by that?" she asked.

"A couple of senators from New England, both of them involved, Nick said, with the Armed Services Committee in Washington, D.C. I saw the secretary of defense. Even a four-star general stopped by."

"Any others?"

"Foreign types. Looked like they were from the Middle East. One guy must have been a sheik."

"You got photos of all of them?" Heather reiterated.

"Every single one. And others. But that's not all."

She waited without much patience.

"Tape recordings," Evans told her. "Nick brought down some real sensitive equipment. Even the Tuskegee 'volunteers' had no idea we were doing this. Microphones are planted all over that area."

"You have the tapes safely stored?"

"Copies are back in my office. Estelle here has a set as well. The originals were put in a safe-deposit box at a bank in Washington, D.C. Nick seemed to be getting ready to use all that stuff. That's why, before you arrived, I couldn't understand why I hadn't heard from him for months . . . now I know."

"This could destroy everything they've accomplished," Heather said. "When the media get finished with it, there will be an outcry that will remake even the cartel's paid puppets into instant traitors."

"Oh yes. And I have proof of something else."

Heather smiled slightly with admiration for this big, gruff man as she asked what that was.

"They no longer use only poor black folk in their experiments," Evans replied. "What they do these days goes beyond that. The guys we're talkin' about have invested billions in the abortion industry."

Heather felt weak quite suddenly. "My husband and I knew that something had to be going on when we first discovered how many babies were aborted *alive,*" she remarked, drawing from snippets of knowledge that she and Nick had pieced together over the years. "They're shipped in portable incubators to God-knows-where."

"Sweden is one place. Medical experiments on live fetuses is accepted practice in a country where socialized medicine rules the roost. I mean, this sort of thing is very big business, which is why there is such brainwashing about abortion."

"If more than a million and a half babies *aren't* aborted, these guys lose mountains of money," Estelle said. "Their dirty dollars are behind those Family Planning Group clinics. After all, the founder's original intention was to concentrate on black babies. It was her homage to the Klan, the Aryans Underground, and other such groups with which she just happened to be in sympathy.

"Babies are used as guinea pigs for radiation, chemical, or whatever other tests their tormenters can dream up. Genetic experimentation here in the United States, in the greatest secrecy, has been using untold numbers of fetuses. And it never gets out through the media because that would be a body blow for the abortionists.

"Now that a president of the United States has lifted *all* restrictions that once outlawed the use of dead fetuses, you will see an increase in abortions on women who will be *paid* for the tiny corpses torn from their own bodies."

"It's disgusting!" Heather agreed. "They're making a profit every step of the way. Each year they might have access to *hundreds of thousands of babies*. And they get *x* number of dollars a head!"

"That's why they gave up on Tuskegee blacks," Evans said, wincing a bit. "As soon as *Roe v. Wade* was sanctioned by the Supreme Court, these guys had access to all the fresh bodies they'd ever need."

"How much of all this information had you managed to get to my husband?" Heather asked.

"Just about everything, I guess, except for most of the abortion stuff."

"The burden Nick carried with him!" she exclaimed. "And he felt he could share none of it with me. . . ."

"Nobody can doubt why that man died, ma'am. The arms dealers have tens of billions of dollars at stake. They have the power to get somebody killed for a few thousand dollars on up, no limit at all. Look at both Kennedys! Or maybe just a few hundred, if it's to a junkie who lives from fix to fix."

"You sound as though you know quite a bit about that sort of thing," Heather told him cautiously.

"Oh, I do, I surely do. I happen to be a widower, ma'am. . . . You see, my wife, Arlene, was killed last year, just after Christmas, of all times for that to happen, when her car was broadsided by an out-of-state college kid driving a year-old Jaguar as he zoomed past a stop sign at a hundred miles an hour.

"Arlene was crushed to death in an instant. I couldn't get her body out in one piece. My men and I had to *scrape* it from the twisted metal. And today all five of those guys have been killed as well."

Heather was about to walk over to Evans and hug him when, with no warning, the entire structure of the mall shook as though it was some mammoth beast that had been mortally wounded.

Clothes racks all around them overturned. Glass partitions shattered. Boxes tumbled off shelves, sprawling their contents on the floor. In a very basic sort of store, the few mannequins in sight were knocked over, hands falling off, heads rolling along the floor like oddly-shaped bowling balls.

Outside, dozens of people had begun to scream a split second before a giant explosion ripped through a pet shop three doors down from the clothing outlet, emptying aquariums, splitting open bird cages, and releasing surviving parakeets and canaries in the mall outside into a kind of precarious freedom.

Evans drew his pistol and ran to the store's entrance.

"A tank!" he yelled as soon as he reached it and saw what was happening. "They've crashed a tank clear through! And they're firing all over the mall, one shell after another. People are—"

He was speaking accurately.

The enormous tank was apparently being directed to fire large shells at regular intervals, from the left to the right of its range, shattering storefronts, sending more glass out in dangerous bursts through the air.

Heather rushed to his side.

"Look! There's Estelle!" she said, her eyes opening wide as she pointed to one side of the monstrous shape that she recognized as an Abrams Attack Vehicle—the word *tank* must have seemed too old-fashioned to the military types. "Nothing you have here can do anything against equipment like that!"

"Mrs. Tazelaar, you just have no idea the kinds of stuff that we have in this mall," Evans told her, winking. "Frankly, we're not known for telling the Feds everything—from the days of moonshine until now."

Estelle had charged out of a sporting goods store, followed by three men. She was carrying two hand grenades while the men were shouldering what looked like a portable missile carrier of some sort.

"Where did you people get that stuff?" Heather asked.

"No comment," Evans replied.

"What is that thing the guys have?"

"It used to be called a bazooka. But it's different . . . capable of a lot more destruction. It carries a small sidewinder."

Some mall customers had managed to go around the back of the tank and get outside. But they didn't go much farther than that. A quick burst of machine-gun fire cut all of them down.

The missile on the carrier was fired, its load tearing off part of the turret, then also ripping a hole through the mall's outer wall as it made contact and exploded, causing a section of the frame holding up the second floor to crumple. Heavy debris poured down on the ground level, burying men, women, and children underneath.

Estelle, yelling like an attacking Sioux brave, climbed up onto the turret, pulled the ring on the grenade she had been holding, and dropped the gray-colored, oblong-shaped object inside, then jumped off and ran as fast as she could.

The tank's specially reinforced metal was so strong that the exploding grenade did nothing other than what Estelle had intended—kill the men inside—with no evidence of outer destruction at all.

"Without that missile," Evans said, shaking his head, "none of us would have had a chance."

"I still don't know how you got it," Heather reminded him.

"It was shipped here by mistake a few months ago. Even the cartel makes that kind of dumb mistake every so often. When we had it in our possession, you can bet we weren't about to give it up."

"I wonder where it was *supposed* to end up?"

"Dunno."

He pointed to the right of the tank, where daylight could be seen.

"Now we've got to contend with whoever on their side is left out there," Evans said, his large frame shuddering.

Curiously, the people who had survived were not panicking, perhaps because they were too dazed to do anything but dig themselves out of the wreckage and then stand and look in confusion around themselves, cuts on their faces and their arms and legs, some with broken ribs, a few blinded by flying shards of glass, others yet buried, a handful not dead but moaning, sobbing.

Estelle took over the job of directing care of the injured, as much as this could be done given the limited resources. A rather small drugstore at the far end of the mall had as yet escaped damage. Directly in front of it, she set up a makeshift hospital of sorts. Painkillers were administered by the druggist and his staff of two. Gauze wrappings, antiseptic sprays, and other needed items quickly ran out.

Sheriff Evans stood guard at the main entrance while another man, armed with a shotgun, took over at a second, smaller one on the other side.

Heather helped with the task of treating scores of cuts and gashes. One man, who had seemed to be only slightly hurt, went through a series of wrenching spasms just after she had applied some salve to an open wound on his left shoulder. Undoubtedly there were internal injuries that she had no experience in diagnosing.

Just as he was coughing up some fluids, which dribbled over his lips and down his chin, he looked at her, pain no longer reflected on his face.

"It's true what we've been taught all these years, every bit of it, you know," he muttered. "Angels . . ."

The man's eyes closed, and his body became limp.

Heather bowed her head.

There was so much more pain for you, my beloved, she prayed. *You were tortured until your heart could endure no more. And then you were just tossed aside!*

She heard Sheriff Evans shouting as though from a very great distance.

"Two helicopters this time," he was saying, risking renewed chaos as he reacted from his own mushrooming panic. "And they're heading straight for us!"

She rushed to where he was standing, looking up at the two shapes that had appeared above the row of trees at the edge of the parking lot.

"Look!" she said, pointing to the left of the Apaches.

Four fighter jets.

The copters turned to face the incoming jets.

"They're going to have to draw the Apaches away from us," Evans remarked in a softer voice. "Otherwise, out of sheer nastiness, the pilots could crash one or two of them into this building. There'd be little hope for any of us if *that* happened!"

One of the Apaches fired at a jet and missed. But a second burst made a direct hit, and the plane crashed into the forest below.

"We need more firepower," Evans said. "What're our guys *doing?*"

People who were able to walk at all gathered behind them.

"There!" one of the women shouted. "Look at that!"

Several other jets approached from behind the Apaches.

The jets fired, virtually in unison.

One of the Apaches was hit immediately in its fuel tank, and it exploded with such force that it almost knocked the second one right out of the sky.

The walls of the mall shook. More glass inside broke. Children cried. Moans of pain and fear filled the air.

Evans leaned over and whispered into Heather's ear.

"Without being too obvious about it," he said, "take in a couple of deep breaths, as though you're sighing with relief, and then tell me if you smell anything."

She did what he suggested, and she knew, then, why he had asked this.

Gas!

Heather nodded discreetly, telling Evans by this motion that she agreed with him about what he himself had detected.

That last wrenching of the mall must have opened up at least some of the gas lines that had been feeding into it. In a very short while others would notice this as well and realize that they were in the greatest danger of all.

As the stunned crowd watched, the remaining Apache shot down one jet, and then a second, followed by another.

Finally, it, too, was hit, though not in the gas-tank area like the other. Instead, two of its blades were sheared off, which proved to be equally devastating, the copter spinning out of control, wobbling like a child's toy in the air, yet the men inside still firing wildly, hitting a dozen or more of the cars in the parking lot, as it headed in a zigzag course that seemed to make collision with the mall inescapable.

"Move it!" Evans shouted. *"Now!"*

The sheriff stepped aside and people pushed past into the open, dozens of them, their expressions showing their fear.

"Look at that," Heather said, smiling.

"Yeah, isn't that great," he agreed. "If only folks acted like that all the time."

Heather had been indicating the injured, none of whom were being forgotten, as other men and women and even teenagers helped them to their feet or lifted the badly hurt and carried them outside.

"Where's Estelle?" Heather shouted, aware that little time was left.

"There!" Evans said, his tone relieved, as he pointed just ahead as their friend was coming into view.

Looking a little foolish, Estelle Breuer approached them, carrying two large bird cages with her. Inside each, oddly unperturbed by the confusion around them, was a multicolored miniature parrot.

"Somehow, I couldn't stand to see anything this helpless be hurt," she said, half apologetically.

"Go! Go!" Evans pleaded, looking frantically at the line of a dozen men, women, and children that remained behind her.

Estelle stepped past the shattered entranceway only a matter of seconds before the Apache collided with the far end of the mall.

Sheriff Amos Evans grabbed Heather and flung her outside just as a wave of solid flame *whooshed* past, carrying him and the remaining group of victims with it, their screams like those of the condemned in hell itself.

180

18

★ ★ ★

Lloyd Brahill had been slightly wounded after Heather fled.

He escaped death by what he admitted later was "the oldest trick in the book"—playing dead. The attackers went right by him. After they were well out of sight, he got to his feet, returned to the highway, and flagged down a car. He was taken to the nearby military base, where he met up with Robert Gridley. The full-fledged response followed almost immediately.

After the attackers were wiped out, hordes of military personnel descended upon the parking lot. Fire-fighting copters and trucks were called in from communities across that county. But there was agreement that no one would be found alive after the various "hot points" throughout the mall were put out and everything cooled down sufficiently that rescue efforts could be made, however unsuccessful these were doomed to be.

"I guess I was able to do something worthwhile for once in my life," Robert Gridley told Heather and Estelle just before the two of them boarded a small Air Force helicopter.

"This isn't the first time you came through," Estelle reassured him. "How about that forest fire years ago?"

He blushed as he thought of that one.

"Well, yes, but this—," he persisted.

"Quiet, guy!" she declared. "This entire area owed much to you before this ever happened."

Heather and Estelle waved good-bye as they climbed on board. In a few seconds, the copter had taken off.

As they flew over what was left of the mall, Estelle did something quite uncharacteristic of her—she started sobbing. Heather cradled the other woman's head in her arms.

"I never realized how quickly everything in my little world could be pulled out from under me," Estelle said as she started to calm down, the surge of emotions passing. "This morning I went to work, and life seemed so predictable. Now it's not yet evening and look at the rubble down there!"

"I felt the same way a few weeks ago," Heather assured her. "That was when I learned what had happened to Nick. Some terrible men were responsible for kidnaping my husband. They tortured him to death and dumped his mangled body seven thousand miles away in a foreign country. He had been left there for days. The lid was closed at his funeral. I couldn't even lean over and kiss him for the last time."

Her arms fell down to her sides. She looked at Estelle, whose own cheeks were covered with tears.

"You need me now, and look what I am doing!" Heather said, deeply ashamed at her behavior.

Lloyd Brahill was sitting in the cockpit, beside the pilot. He leaned back over his seat, and said, "Take a look below. . . ."

The two of them glanced over a small round window in front of them.

The village.

"Can you fly a little lower?" Brahill requested.

The pilot accommodated him.

Heather and Estelle could see a stream of ambulances entering the center of the village, along with several military jeeps.

"You're getting help for them!" Heather said.

"It's about time, isn't it?" Brahill remarked.

The two women glanced at one another.

"Can we land near there?" Heather asked.

"Don't worry about them," he responded. "They'll be given first-class care now. *You* need a hospital now. Both of you do."

"I've got to see if one of the women is going to be all right," Heather persisted. "Her name's—"

"Ophelia," added Estelle, finishing the sentence for her.

"Impossible," Brahill insisted. "It's—"

The pilot was looking at him.

"Isn't it?" he asked.

"There's a clearing a couple of miles away," the pilot suggested. "I could radio down to one of the jeeps, get them to meet us there."

"Heather . . . ," Brahill started to say.

"I heard," she told him. "Will you authorize it, Lloyd, please?"

Brahill hesitated, knowing how weak both of them were.

"All right," he relented. "But I mean it: take fifteen minutes, no longer. Is that understood?"

"Aye, aye, sir," Heather said, kidding him.

In just a short while the copter was on the ground, a jeep waiting for them.

The scene before Heather was one of pathetic sights and sounds. She saw half a dozen dark-gray canvas body bags lined up to one side. Emerging from crumbling, threadbare homes, soldiers were carrying men and women so frail in appearance that they seemed to belong in the midst of famine-stricken Ethiopia or Somalia, not in the United States—skin stretched over protruding bones, eyes bloodshot, cheeks pinched in, mouths filled with rotting teeth that were visible between pale, thin lips.

She heard people moaning, some gasping for air, their lungs damaged just as surely as though they had smoked three packs of cigarettes per day. Others were coughing violently. A few bled through the pores in their skin. Several, showing their emotions readily, were thanking the men carrying them away from that ghastly place, most of the rest muttering a ragged but emotional "Amen!"

Just a handful seemed reluctant to leave.

At first Heather found that unfathomable and said so to Estelle, who replied, "I can understand your reaction. Remember one fact, though: These poor souls were thrown into this nightmare because they *trusted* government types and were foolish enough to ask few questions. The scared ones have no way of knowing—and others *are* scared whether they show it or not—I mean, *absolutely* knowing that they won't be betrayed again, exchanging this hell for another that might be even worse."

"Even worse?" Heather repeated. "How could that be?"

"Look at it this way: Before Tuskegee entered their lives, they were as poor as you can become in this country. That's why they were drawn to Tuskegee in the first place: the promise of money and proper medical care that was dangled in front of each and every one of them. They desperately wanted to escape the degradation of the way they had been living at the time. For them, in those days, it couldn't have been worse, they thought.

"The Tuskegee Project changed that. It showed these people that the quality of life, no matter how abysmal, could become worse, much worse, in one way or another. I would wager that everyone here now looks back on the old days, those days of poverty and despair, with some wistfulness, for what they have today makes what they gave up seem like heaven in comparison."

She paused, then added, "That, my friend, is why they fear the possibility that it could be worse for them if they leave this place, as awful as it is. They have forty years of proof to back that up!"

The ones who had to be coaxed or forced from that village passed by Heather and Estelle as soldiers took their hands and helped them into an ambulance. An elderly man, pure white hair topping a face of weathered black skin, with scars on the forehead and cheeks and an old gash in his chin, saw Heather and turned toward her for a moment.

"You was with Ophelia yesterday," he said, his eyes sparkling. "She be so glad to see you."

"Where is she, sir?"

"Back in her house, gettin' ready."

For Heather, the huts looked enough alike for her to forget the one in which the old woman had lived.

"Can you tell me which it is?" she asked.

The ancient human being in front of her slowly raised his

185

hand, which was shaking, and pointed across the dirt street to the hut in the middle.

"There," he said. "There she be now, probably on her knees, raising her voice in praise to the Almighty as she petitions Him for herself, for all of us."

Heather reached out, cupped her hands around that unsteady one of his, then leaned forward and kissed him on the forehead.

"How old are you, sir?" she asked.

"Three score years, ma'am."

"You're only—!" she started to say then bit off the rest of the words.

"I look four score and ten, I know that, surely I do. It's the medicine they gave me. Finally, though, they stopped doing it."

"Why?" Heather asked.

"Couldn't find no more veins to use."

He held out both arms. The flesh was sunken, the veins collapsed. He rolled up his tattered old slacks, and it was the same on his legs.

"I tried to fight, to say that what they were doin' was wrong, that they had no right. But then they showed me a sheet of paper I was 'posed to have signed. And they said it was no use for me to protest 'cause they was the government, and I could never win."

Estelle was standing to Heather's left, Lloyd Brahill to her right.

"This is my attorney, my friend," she said. "He's going to see that you're protected, that nobody experiments on you again."

"But where is they gonna to put us?" the old man asked.

"I don't know," Heather admitted.

186

"In one of those low-income developments? They is like prisons. Some even have bars on the windows."

"I just don't—"

He withdrew his hands from her own and turned away, his eyes suddenly filling with fear.

"Please . . . don't worry about anything," Heather said, "you've got good people to take care of you now. Please—"

He looked at her once more, an expression of hopelessness on his face, and then he stepped slowly into the back of the ambulance.

"It will take a long while for them to adjust," Brahill whispered. "And it will never be a very good life for any of these people, I'm afraid."

"He didn't seem to be at all pleased by the thought of staying in a housing development. That's strange, after living as he has been doing for so long."

"Not so strange when you consider that the old guy's more than likely heard the stories about crime—drugs, rapes, robberies, the rest. Those images are in his mind, and he's terrified by them."

"We owe you so much," Heather said.

"This war against the cartel is just in the early stages. Nick thought it would take a long time to clear out the scum who have been at the center of all this, perhaps years to correct the evils. He was right, Heather. We can't rejoice just yet, not for a long time, in fact. We had better get used to living our lives in danger."

He put his hands on her shoulders and turned her around so that she faced the dirt street and the huts across from them.

"Go to Ophelia now," he said. "I'll take care of every- body else."

"Estelle?" she said. "Are you ready?"

187

"I wonder if I am," the other woman confessed reluctantly. "It's been a long time. She's always seemed old to me, one of those people, well, you wonder if they were *ever* young. Now she really is old, and sick as well, and I don't know if my conscience can face the lost years, the years when I never came to spend time with Ophelia, to do more than pray for her from a distance."

"But what kept you away?" Heather asked.

"Shame!" Estelle blurted out. "I was ashamed of her black skin and her rags and the smell of this place, the poverty of it."

She was shaking as she spoke.

"I can express all the outrage imaginable over their plight here, but how many people have I kept from a glimpse of the truth about *them* because of what it would reveal about *me*? I mean, I had a *black* mother, and she died horribly. And now my *black* grandmother's days are dwindling, and yet, until just a couple of hours ago, only you and Gridley and Sheriff Evans are aware of my connection with all this.

"I have to go with you to that dreary little shack, oh, how I know that, Heather! I have to face that woman and hold her in my arms, and beg her somehow to forgive me. But . . . but it's so hard, it's so hard to look inside myself and admit that I don't like what I see!"

Her eyes were bloodshot as she added, "The very worst part is that these people suffered years longer as a result of me. I could have lifted the lid a long time ago! But I refused to let most of the white folk around here find out that I was a nigger's child!"

"But Evans knew. Gridley, too. Why them?"

"Because we've been friends for most of our lives. I had to trust someone."

"And they went along with you?"

"They had . . . until your husband came here, until he told us the full extent of what was happening here and elsewhere in the United States and so many other places around the world. We knew we couldn't ignore it any longer. We still had some part of our consciences that hadn't withered away to nothing."

Estelle's expression had changed into one of eagerness.

"We all were getting ready to expose the whole thing," she said, her eyes sparkling as she licked her lips.

"Without Stelzfuss having any idea that this was the case," Heather remarked, catching some of the other's excitement. "And with his daughter at the center of it!"

"Exactly. Thank God there's a copy of the file safe in that bank."

Heather fell silent.

"Thinking about Nick?" Estelle guessed.

"That I am," she replied. "He started a kind of tornado."

They hugged one another, then turned and faced the hut in front of them.

"I'll be right here," Estelle said. "Would you go in and get her?"

Heather nodded.

"I hope she doesn't hate me, Heather. But I don't see how she couldn't . . . after all this time."

"Sometimes love just won't die. Sometimes it's so strong, so deep that nothing can stand against it."

Heather walked across the dirt street and up the cinder block steps, pausing for a moment on the bare, rotting wood porch.

Ophelia's voice.

She heard it coming from inside.

"Lord Jesus, Lord Jesus, Lord Jesus" was being spoken over and over.

As Heather entered, she saw Ophelia on her knees, head bowed, hands held out in front of her, palms upward. Around her was the sum total of her material possessions—a couple of chairs, an old table, a wood-burning stove, a few pieces of clothing folded neatly on top of that table.

Back home, I used to become upset if my electronic dishwasher needed service and I had to do everything by hand, Heather thought uncomfortably. *If I had a run in my nylon stockings, or a smudge on a blouse bought just days before . . . !*

She remembered one night when the electricity went out because it was a time of extreme muggy summer heat and demand proved extraordinarily high.

Several hours had passed before power was restored.

I sweltered without our air-conditioning. Nick was away on an assignment. If he had been with me, he would have been my conscience and restrained my anger. But he was nowhere around, and I lost it, calling the electric company operators every half hour, demanding to know what was happening. They all tried to be as polite as possible but I lost my Christian testimony that night.

All because a convenience to which I had grown accustomed wasn't available to me when I wanted it to be. I made some blameless people miserable. And I didn't sleep well that night, the Holy Spirit prodding my conscience again and again.

Now here are dozens of people with far less than I've ever had, trying far more earnestly to be happy. . . .

"Ophelia?" she spoke finally, with some hesitancy. "We've got to take you away from this place right away, dear."

"My home," the old woman replied without turning to face her.

"I know that, but there's something better waiting for you, something much better. Please believe me."

Ophelia finally stood, with great difficulty.

"I do believe you," she said, "'cause the Lord told me you could be trusted, that you're one of His."

"I am," Heather told her. "I have been for many years. So was Nick."

"Praise Jesus!"

She pointed to the dresses. "I washed them as best I could in the stream in back. They isn't much, but they is all I have."

"I'm going to get some brand-new ones for you."

"I've never had a new dress," Ophelia mused. "It must be wonderful not wearing old things, torn things for a change."

She smiled weakly, with some embarrassment over the threadbare cloth of her dress, the faded plaid colors.

"Being old and hurtin' is bad," she added. "Being old and hurtin' and poor is a little hint of hell."

Ophelia took Heather's hand for support and started to walk with great hesitancy toward the open door.

"My bag and my Bible," she said, stopping. "I can't forget them."

Heather saw both on a wobbly little round table next to a very old rocking chair. As she picked up the Bible and then the bag, which was quite small, little more than a tattered duffel bag in miniature, the contents were visible since Ophelia hadn't remembered to use the zipper and close it.

Two other dresses, a toothbrush, a mirror.

"Isn't there anything else you'll want?" she asked the old woman.

"Plenty that I want . . . nothin' that I have."

The two of them walked slowly outside. Holding the worn

Bible with one hand, Ophelia raised her other one over her eyes to block the sun momentarily.

"Someone there?" she asked, thinking that she had seen a form in front of her but not certain.

"Grandmama . . . ," Estelle called to her.

Ophelia stood still.

"Who are you?" she asked a little nervously.

Estelle walked up to her, stroking the old woman's withered cheek gently with the fingers of her left hand.

"Why do you call me grandmama?" Ophelia asked, squinting.

"I'm Estelle . . . your grandchild."

Ophelia's eyes opened wide as she tilted her head slightly, examining this woman who was trying to confuse her by making such a claim.

"You're *not* that child," she said. "Estelle's been stayin' away for many years. She never come back like this, not now. I'm gonna go to be with Jesus without ever seeing my granddaughter again."

Anger flashed across Ophelia's deeply lined face. "Estelle's mother died in my arms," she went on. "She had pain, so much pain, from what they did to her. That man!"

She shook a tiny vein-lined fist in front of her. "I had to bury my daughter myself out among the trees. Couldn't provide nothin' but a wood marker. It keeps rotting away. I've been replacin' it every few years."

Words started to choke in her throat. "Alone here . . . for . . . so long. Old Elijah loved me . . . but that's all. No one else. The others had their own worlds of suffering wrapped around them. One after the other died, and yet I hung on, though I don't know how."

She faced Estelle. "You ain't no daughter of mine," she said. "My daughter's—"

"Listen, Grandmama," Estelle interrupted. "I've got a pretty good voice. I do some singing in churches. I know your favorite hymn, and I'm gonna sing it now. Maybe you'll believe me then."

Ophelia turned toward Heather. "This woman's crazy," she remarked. "I gotta leave this place. I gotta get me away from her!"

She started to walk falteringly toward the nearest ambulance. Estelle looked at Heather.

"Ophelia's going to leave me," she said. "Singing an old hymn won't be enough. I know it won't."

"In its own way, this is nearly as difficult as escaping death in a blown-up shopping mall," Heather admitted. "But you may never have another chance."

Estelle closed her eyes, trying to remember the words.

"Abide . . . with me," she began uncertainly, "fast . . . falls the eventide."

Abruptly, Ophelia cocked her head as those words reached her.

"The darkness deepens," Estelle continued, "Lord, with me abide."

Ophelia stood without moving for a moment, tears filling her eyes, and then her thin, dry lips moved slowly.

"When other helpers fail and comforts flee," she joined in, her raspy voice gaining strength, "Help of the helpless, O abide with me."

Other villagers, already into the various ambulances or approaching them, paused for a few seconds, listened, and then started to sing together in an impromptu chorus.

One of the soldiers looked in Lloyd Brahill's direction.

"Go ahead," he said a little uncomfortably.

Most of them took off their helmets and added their voices.

Heather walked over to Brahill and nudged him with her elbow as she whispered, "Let's join in."

"My voice stinks," he told her. "It would be much too embarrassing."

"Nonsense. There's actually something to be said for making a joyful noise every so often, Lloyd."

He smiled, nodding.

"Nick once told me that you could get him to do anything," he told her, "but don't say I didn't warn you!"

And then, minutes later, it was over, all the verses sung, the moment had passed, and the exodus from that place continued.

Ophelia stretched out her arms and Estelle nearly stumbled into them.

"Oh, Grandmama," she said, "you're so thin."

"Eighty-five pounds," Ophelia replied sadly, "the same weight your mother was when she died."

"Please forgive me," Estelle begged.

"I just pray, child, that someday you won't be ashamed of me any more."

Estelle placed a finger on those ancient lips. "No longer," she said, "no longer, Grandmama."

Everyone stopped looking at the two, giving them some fleeting moment of privacy, as much as could be so out there in the open.

"Lloyd?" Heather spoke after turning away. "What can we do to help?"

"It would be awkward to give the old woman any kind of special treatment," he acknowledged.

"But you don't know the whole story," she protested.

"Go ahead but make it quick."

She told him briefly what she had learned about Ophelia and Estelle's mother.

"I see what you mean," he said, letting out a long sigh. "I suppose exceptions can be made in almost any situation."

"What *can* you do?" Heather persisted.

"Have Ophelia remain behind with Estelle."

"But doesn't she need special treatment because of Tuskegee?"

"Oh, she does," Brahill agreed completely. "Every one of these people will need it for the rest of their lives. But I don't see why we couldn't put Ophelia in a decent motel near here for a few days before she's taken to Walter Reed Hospital. After that, it might be that Estelle can be there with her for awhile."

"She doesn't have much money."

"The federal government undoubtedly can be coerced into paying for whatever is needed. But if I'm overruled along the bureaucratic chain of command, then I personally will assume every dollar of expense."

"You're a lot like Nick."

"And *you* are everything he said you were."

He started to bite his lower lip, which was not characteristic of him.

"What is it?" she asked.

"After the hymn singing and their reconciliation, we come back to another kind of reality." His expression was sombre.

"They'll never leave that hospital, will they?" she stated as much as asked.

"I doubt it, Heather. Oh, there may be a few brief respites when they experience a little pleasure visiting Longwood Gardens or going to the shore perhaps, but basically, they will live the rest of their lives in an institution, with tests being conducted daily . . . the awful legacy that Tuskegee has left behind.

"I don't think Ophelia, for example, has more than a few months, or perhaps only weeks left. I'm not a doctor, but I've been involved as an attorney in *many* medical cases. Her body is wrecked. The doctors can add *some* time to her life but that's all. There's no way in the world that they can save her."

19

★ ★ ★

Heather didn't talk much during the early moments of the helicopter trip back to Washington, D.C. She was thinking about Nick and Estelle and Ophelia and other men and women over the past few days, including the grotesquely fat creature named Erik Stelzfuss who was behind the nightmare.

That man has destroyed many thousands of lives over the past several decades, probably since well before both of the Kennedy assassinations, she told herself. *Now he's either dead from those burns or else he's hired the best surgeons he could find and is having them patch him back together.*

"Will Stelzfuss ever be found?" she asked out loud.

"There are some leads," Lloyd Brahill declared. "But who knows? If Colombian drug lord Pablo Escobar can escape from prison so easily, what does that say about the ability of someone who's already on the loose to *avoid* capture, a guy whose power makes even Escobar's seem rather puny."

Both fell silent again until the helicopter was just

a few minutes away from Washington National Airport.

"What about Mengele?" Heather asked.

"What about him?" Brahill replied.

"Wasn't there something about him being sighted in Hawaii?"

"There have been many such reports, in one country or another, for years, Heather," he offered. "Supposedly the grave of Josef Mengele was found a couple of years ago and his remains identified."

"Do you believe that?"

"Why shouldn't I?"

"He was mentioned in the MM file. And that agent I was telling you about—you know, Weatherby—was convinced of his continuing survival."

"I realize that. But it doesn't mean Weatherby was right. I even heard some talk about Mengele breaking away from Paperclip to do studies of his own."

. . . studies of his own.

Both of them felt chills at the implications in that statement.

"When was that?" she asked.

"I can't be sure, but I think it was about the time of JFK's assassination."

"Interesting coincidence," Heather mused.

"It is. Hey, there's that tone of yours," Brahill said. "I mean, are you hinting at something?"

She shook her head. "Paperclip and Stelzfuss and Mengele all are connected with the cartel. Weatherby said that the cartel was behind protecting Mengele ever since the Argentine government got cold feet."

Brahill's manner changed.

"Keep talking, Heather," he urged.

"Nick showed a major interest in Mengele before he got that file. He had some idea that, one day, that devil would cross his path."

"And Nick would be the one to capture him?"

"Wishful thinking, I know, but he hated the idea that *any-one* like that would escape punishment."

"Here's something else," he added.

"You're not laughing at me anymore?"

"That's right. Listen to this, Heather, and tell me the first thought that enters your thought."

"Go ahead. . . ."

"Mengele's driving passion always has been experimentation on the human body," Brahill explained. "This Erik Stelzfuss you saw running into the woods, if he's not dead, needs help desperately. Mengele is old now, but he's still got a kind of demonic genius."

"And if we're right, he's already on Stelzfuss's payroll!"

"He was when he was with the project."

"Even if he has left and is off on his own, he must be getting funds from somewhere," she pointed out.

"And Stelzfuss is unlikely to burn any bridges with someone like that."

"Hey, you wanted me to tell you the first thought that enters my mind. About what, Lloyd?"

"I'm slowly getting to the point. Remember, I'm a lawyer, and I think like one. That's why law is so complicated these days. Too many guys like me have put in their two cents' worth over the years."

Heather tried to wait patiently, though with some amusement at her friend's long-windedness.

"Did you know that Mengele was the one behind those infamous lamp shades," Brahill said portentously.

"The kind made of human skin?"

"Precisely! He was quite adept at lifting off just enough layers to make sure that, when the skin dried, it wouldn't go to pieces because of being too thin."

Heather could feel her heart beating faster.

"You're sweating, my dear," Brahill observed. "I bet you've caught a glimpse of where I'm heading, haven't you?"

She gulped a couple of times before saying, "If he is expert at taking human skin *off*, then, unknown to the rest of us, he might have become just as good at—"

"—grafting it back on!" he finished, his voice nearly at a shout. "Stelzfuss will be needing heavy-duty plastic surgery right from the start, thanks to you, and I'm not talking a nose job or a little tuck here and there. He knows Mengele well enough to understand that he needn't fear betrayal from the man. So he is placing his life in a maniac's hands because, at least, Mengele is *his* maniac!"

Brahill took out a handkerchief from a pocket in his slacks and wiped his face with it as he added, "Where we find Josef Mengele, there's a strong chance that, given our scenario, Erik Stelzfuss will be right at his side."

Brahill's shoulders slumped.

"What's wrong, Lloyd?" Heather asked.

"All the efforts of every appropriate branch or department of government in this country, Israel, England, and others over the years to find Megele have resulted in failure. Mengele has never been found, unless you count that gravesite.

"If he *is* alive, look at how cleverly he stopped any further pursuit. The CIA, then, was tricked. So was the National Security Council. Not to mention the State Department. It would take a miracle for something to turn up. A cold trail in a case that has been closed for several years hardly inspires optimism."

"Unless . . . ," Heather started to say before pausing.

"All right, it's my turn. A light just went on. Explain."

"If Stelzfuss and his cohorts increasingly feel cornered, they may behave more and more often in a desperate manner," she went on. "Bombings, more assassinations, other acts of terrorism."

"And desperation breeds carelessness—making them easier to trace."

"I mean, Lloyd, what else could any of us call the attack they waged against the shopping mall?"

She looked at her hands. They were shaking.

"I was the one they were after," she said.

He placed his hands over hers.

"I was going to get you on the ground before I told you this," he said.

"Tell me what?" Heather asked.

"That you can't return to your home for awhile. We've got to keep you safe, with twenty-four-hour security. You'll be living elsewhere for awhile."

"There's something else, isn't there?"

"I'm afraid so. . . . They must have searched it thoroughly for Nick's file. When they couldn't find it, they trashed *everything* inside."

"No!" she screamed. "There was so much I had to remind me of Nick."

"Some of your belongings may be intact, but much more is just debris."

He looked at her, his expression intent.

"You can't go back, Heather," he said. "You're going to have to completely relocate. We'll try to gather up whatever we can that might be worthwhile. Could you give us a list of some things you might want?"

She nodded, hearing him but not entirely focussed on what had been said.

Nick gone, she thought. *Our home off-limits. I'm in the care of someone I hardly know. Oh Lord, if there ever was a Valley of the Shadow of Death . . . please, please, help me get through this, dear Jesus. I need Thee more now than ever before.*

20

★ ★ ★

It was a nice enough condominium, quite posh by most standards, painted a cheerful pastel yellow, a beige shingle roof, a kitchen, living room, dining room, and half bath on the first floor, and two bedrooms with two full baths on the second, the furniture mostly in French provincial.

"Do you like it?" Lloyd Brahill asked.

Heather did and told him so.

"That's just great," he said, beaming.

"But my clothes," she reminded him, still wearing the torn and dirty blouse and jeans she had gotten at the mall. "Is *everything* gone, Lloyd?"

"All of it," he confessed. "I hate to spoil the surprise, but I have to suggest that you look upstairs in the walk-in closet and the bureau before you become too concerned. They're in the bedroom to your left."

Her eyes opened wide, a broad smile crossing her face.

"Like my wife," he added good-naturedly. "Tell her about new clothes and, well, she's bursting with joy."

Heather laughed and then hurried up the stairs to the master bedroom. The closet was large enough to be considered almost a room in itself. And it was bursting with clothes—blouses and skirts and dresses of every style and color. On the floor were at least a dozen pairs of shoes.

In the bureau were underwear, handkerchiefs, nylon stockings.

And a four-by-five-inch color snapshot of Nick with his arm around her as they sat on an isolated Hawaiian black sand beach, the turquoise-blue Pacific in front of them.

She noticed that the edges of the photo were burnt and curled slightly, but the main part was very much intact.

Heather hurried back downstairs, holding the photo out in front of her.

"It was all we could find," Brahill told her regretfully. "It's not much, I know. But frankly, the men responsible were strictly professional at what they were supposed to do. They left quite a pile of rubble, Heather."

"But all those clothes!" she exclaimed. "I don't know what to say."

"No one at the agency had any idea, really, what styles you prefer, or what colors you really like. So, a bunch of us got together with our wives and brainstormed. I hope we're not too far off."

She hugged him.

"Everything seems fine. I'll learn to like *every* piece, and I'll treasure it because of what this all represents, Lloyd!"

"Why don't you shower and change now?" he suggested. "There are some things you need to know."

"About what?"

"Oh, the couple next door, the family across the street—things like that, crucial to your safety."

"Everybody's connected with the agency, aren't they?"

"No, that's not quite the case. There are people from *several* agencies and departments, only those who could be trusted. We wanted to take no chances of any kind."

He grabbed ahold of her shoulder and turned her around to face the stairs. "No more talk for now," he commanded. "Relax. Try on some new clothes after you've showered. Take your time. I'll be right here making some phone calls. I might throw together a couple of sandwiches, too. You're probably real hungry about now. I know that I am."

Heather kissed him on the cheek before she sprinted up the steps.

The shower invigorated Heather. And putting on clean clothes helped as well, especially the cheerful lavender dress that she had picked out. She could almost feel that the chaos was permanently ended and that she was finally safe. But then she also realized that this was self-deception.

I am in a strange house, however beautiful it is, she told herself. *But the neighborhood is nothing more than an armed camp. And I cannot return to my old home nor to my husband or my best friend. I have hope of ever seeing only one of them— dear Becky, wherever she is, if her captors haven't killed her by now.*

Trembling, Heather sat down on the edge of the queen-size canopy bed.

There's no telling when they'll try again with me, or where, or how. No longer can I go on a simple trip—even to the supermarket—without wondering if I will be walking into a trap.

The phone on the nightstand rang and instinctively she reached out to answer it, then stopped as her fingers started to close around the receiver.

205

Every phone call must be screened, she thought. *Every package delivered to this house has to be checked.*

For how long?

As she stood and examined herself in a full-length mirror on the wall next to the bathroom, that question assaulted her.

For months . . . or years?

A knock at the bedroom door made her scream out.

"It's me, Heather," Brahill called in to her. "Are you decent?"

"Yes . . . come in," she told him.

As he opened the door and walked in, he apologized for startling her.

"My fault," she said. "I was standing here feeling sorry for myself, and I wasn't thinking of anything or anyone else."

"Self-pity isn't unusual after someone has been through the series of traumas that you have had," he reassured her. "It often happens to patients who have had massive heart attacks and survived."

"They aren't grateful to be alive?"

"Oh, that's the initial reaction," he explained. "But, soon enough, another sets in. They've been confronted with their mortality. They've come so close to death that they realize it could happen again. It no longer is a distant thunder, loud and threatening but kept away by some miracle from God."

Could that be the case with me, Lord? she thought. *Are You trying to get through to me about my life so that I will change it in some way? I'll listen, Lord. I just need to understand, to hear You a little more clearly.*

"Could it be, Lloyd," she mused out loud, "that I am being reminded how precious life is, that I should be spending it honoring God whenever and wherever I can? Is that what you're trying to tell me?"

"Right on the money, Heather."

"But I'm a Christian, Lloyd. I shouldn't *have* to be taught such things. I have been a believer for more than half my life thus far. I feel almost like a failure if God finds it necessary to teach me like a child."

"Wrong. Christians are fallible human beings. They have basically the same emotions as everybody else. What you fear is not what will happen *after* death. What you fear is . . . let's put it this way . . . the *process* that gets you there."

She stood, hugging herself tightly, her head bowed just a bit, thinking over what he had said.

"Being a Christian also doesn't exempt you from sorrow," he went on. "You've lost Nick. You've lost Becky. And other people who have tried to help you have died along the way. I am amazed that you've not completely fallen apart in the aftermath of all this."

He pointed to a high-backed chair opposite the bed.

"Would you sit down for a moment?" he spoke softly.

"It's that phone call you got, isn't it? That's why you came up here."

"Heather, I have some great news for you."

She sat down, trying to feel more relaxed.

"All right, Lloyd, go ahead and tell me."

"We found Mengele!" he declared with real excitement. "And we think Stelzfuss is right there with him."

He smiled broadly. "To have two monsters like them under the same roof and accessible to us can only be called a bona fide miracle. If Mengele has been with Stelzfuss all these years, no wonder we ran into so many dead ends trying to find him. It seems that Mengele has had more than just a few old friends hiding him away. It's been the cartel all along."

"Becky . . . ," he said simply. "Becky has been spotted with them.

Heather let out a scream of utter surprise and joy and started to get to her feet, but he held his palms out.

"Sit still," he went on. "There's more."

He sat down on the edge of the bed.

"It's really amazing. Apparently they're holding an emergency conference."

"The cartel?"

"Exactly. It's in Hawaii. We've spotted members of the Giambelli family."

"The Mafia's involved?"

"You bet it is. Some terrorist leaders are there as well. Escobar's top lieutenant has joined them. The list keeps on growing. But one of the most shocking discoveries is how many German industrialists are involved.

"*That* tidbit could affect relations with Germany for a long time to come. We've suspected that the government's been ignoring the cartel's influence on the one hand and making sanctimonious public pronouncements on the other."

"And you can arrest them all."

"We can try. It will be like waging an assault against Saddam Hussein. They've got major-league protection. The only consolation is that they are on the windward side of Oahu and aren't near any real population centers."

Heather fell silent.

"I want to be there!" she declared. "I want Becky to know that I am all right and that nothing will be allowed to separate us ever again."

"Impossible!" Brahill protested. "It will be war, Heather. What you've seen, what you've experienced until now, is only a hint."

"I *want* to be there," she pressed. "I want to see those two men either captured or killed. If Mengele had anything at all to do with Nick's—"

"He probably did. But Heather, I can't possibly allow this."

"Then I will go on my own! Becky is all I have left. It will be better for her if—"

"After a certain hour, all commercial air flights to and from all the islands will be temporarily halted," Brahill interrupted futilely.

"Then I'll hire a private plane."

"Heather, clear away all that haze in your mind. Any such plane could be shot down. That's just plain nuts. Forgive me for saying so, but it is."

"Nuts or not, I want to go, Lloyd."

Brahill stood and started pacing in front of her.

"You're ignoring the danger," he argued. "You could be—"

"Killed? Of course. But until I know for certain that the men who murdered Nick have been dealt with, I will have no peace. I might as well be dead myself."

"But you could wait on the mainland. It would be much more prudent for me to call you when everything's under control."

"No! If they're alive, I want to be able to walk up to both of them and tell them how much I loved Nick, and, if I had a knife or a gun, I would kill first one, then the other, right on the spot."

She saw his expression as he looked at her, saw that he began to understand how serious she was, how deeply she *needed* to do what she had said.

"That's a little of what worries me," Brahill declared.

"That I might lose control?"

Roger Elwood

"That you might decide it's not enough to see Mengele and Stelzfuss handcuffed and being led off to a federal prison, where you can't control the outcome."

"I'm not saying I would. I'd like to think that I had more self-control. But could you blame me if I did something like that? How many other murderers are still alive, years after they were apprehended?

"Remember Gacy who murdered more than thirty young men and buried them under his house? He hasn't been executed. He eats three meals a day, has all his clothes provided for him, all his medical needs cared for. And taxpayers like the parents and girlfriends of the victims are footing the bill, as Nick used to say."

Dark memories were surfacing, memories of a time when reports were proliferating from Los Angeles—men and women slaughtered, and no suspect in sight. And then the alleged murderer was captured, with a great deal of fanfare.

"What about the Night Stalker case?" Heather reminded him. "Nick was hoping to persuade the agency to let him take a little time and investigate why, years later, Richard Ramirez hadn't yet been executed by the State of California."

Brahill stopped pacing, spun around, and faced her.

"Corruption, period," he agreed. "You know that. I know it. Dirty money warming the palms of public officials totally without principle. That's probably what an investigator of Nick's caliber would have uncovered. I can't argue with you there, Heather."

"Tell me then," she persisted. "How can we be sure that it won't happen again with Mengele and Stelzfuss? Look at how many puppets those two have! Will there be some clever bit of plea bargaining that reduces their punishment?"

"What you're asking is justice, I know. In today's world,

that can never be guaranteed. I mean, we can't be *sure* that they'll get what they deserve. But there *is* a difference between this case and the one involving the Night Stalker or Gacy, for that matter."

"What's that?"

"Me."

"Nick used to tell me that you had much more influence than anybody could have guessed."

He narrowed his eyes as he said quite seriously, "Believe it, Heather. In fact, not even Nick himself knew the full story."

He smiled reassuringly.

"That's why I said what I did. These men, if that's what we must call them, won't wiggle off the hook, no matter how smart their own attorneys are."

21

★ ★ ★

"I'm just not going to let you do this, Heather. I can't see that Nick would ever have approved either. And there is no way you're going to change my mind!"

Letting herself enjoy that recollection, Heather pulled the drapes aside and opened the sliding-glass doors as Lloyd Brahill's words repeated themselves in her mind. She was on the twenty-second floor of the Diamond-Head side of the Sheraton Waikiki hotel. The clear Pacific remained as it had been over the years, without change, unspoiled by pollution, as clear and beautiful as the first time Nick and she had stayed at the hotel, on that floor, in that same room.

We could not speak, she remembered. *We could only hold one another, breathe in the sweet-scented air, and thank God for bringing us to that moment.*

A mental image of Becky came to mind as well, for she knew how much her friend had wanted to go to Hawaii but never got the chance, before or after her own husband's death.

I told you enough to make you eager to spend time here. Oh, Becky, here I am again, and so are you, but—

She heard a sound and opened her eyes, losing that image of the two of them.

An exotic bird, with wide tail feathers that were twice as long as its body, had landed on the part-concrete, part-iron railing that surrounded the balcony. Sitting quietly, only a breeze stirring its bright red and blue and yellow feathers, it seemed content to do nothing but study her, its crest folded back peacefully against the top of its head.

"Do you want something to eat?" she asked.

The bird showed no alarm at the sound of her voice. It let out a single musical note, as though in response to her question, and then was quiet again.

Heather remembered a small Danish that had been left over from breakfast, and she went back into the room to retrieve it. As she was reaching for the pastry, she noticed that the television set was still on. While standing outside, lost in her memories of times with Nick, she had forgotten about it.

The news announcer was talking about rumors involving the possible closing of the Honolulu International Airport, an action that was certain to cause havoc within the islands. A naval blockade also seemed likely, to be set up around Oahu, with the help of ships stationed at Pearl Harbor.

"Extraordinary!" the announcer declared. "The Coast Guard also may be called into action, and being considered is a constant series of flights by fighter planes from one end of the island to the other."

He leaned toward the camera. "After nearly half a century, Josef Mengele, we are led to believe, finally has been cornered!" he said breathlessly. "But that is only part of the story, of course. Somewhere on this island, as I speak, are reputed mob bosses, arms merchants, and drug cartel chieftains from all over the world.

"No one but the federal authorities know for sure what is going on. But let me ask: Is there a connection with the mainland's big story of a few days ago—the leveling of an East Coast shopping mall by the renegade pilots of two fully equipped Apache helicopters? Sources indicate that the answer may be yes!"

Someone handed him a sheet of paper. The announcer's eyes widened as he skimmed the contents.

"As unbelievable as this may sound," he spoke, "everything from the assassinations of John and Robert Kennedy to the death of Marilyn Monroe somehow could be part of this story! We will keep you posted."

The news bulletin gave way to a rerun of "Murphy Brown," which Heather switched off immediately.

"There goes the myth of governmental secrecy!" Heather growled in disgust, knowing how earnestly Lloyd Brahill and others were trying to maintain the element of surprise. Now, having been tipped off, the cartel's insiders were unlikely to hang around for very long.

Oh Lord, I hope that Lloyd has heard this and is prepared for contingency action, Heather prayed.

She heard the bird on the balcony railing suddenly start squawking and saw a strand of rope out of the corner of her eye.

A chill raced through her body.

She decided to dash for the corridor.

Behind her, she heard someone land on the balcony and start to run inside toward her.

Heather fumbled with the lock on the door leading into the corridor and managed to open it. As she headed outside, the intruder grabbed her neck with both his hands and started to pull her back into the room. She kicked backward with one foot and caught him in the groin, then kicked again, and he doubled over, dropping to his knees.

A struggle next door!

She heard the sounds of a table being overturned, glass breaking, and loud voices, followed by two gunshots.

The secret service agent stationed next door, blond-haired and in his early thirties, stumbled through her doorway, clutching his chest and falling at her feet. He reached up toward her. In his hand was a pistol, which she grabbed.

"Use it!" he cried.

Heather stood, frozen, for a moment. Then she ran toward the elevator at the end of the corridor. Someone with a stocking pulled over his face and dressed in a jumpsuit burst out directly behind her.

She turned, saw him raise what looked like a large black Luger toward her. Remembering a move that Nick once had demonstrated, she dropped to her stomach, groaning from the impact on the carpeted concrete floor, and fired twice in his direction. One shot caught him in the shoulder, the other in his leg.

An elevator was already at that floor. The door *swooshed* open instantly, and she hurried inside.

The door was still open, after several seconds.

Close! Close! her mind screamed as she pushed the button repeatedly.

Heather's original attacker dashed out into the corridor and headed toward her. He had a pistol of his own. As he ran, with both hands folded around it, he aimed the weapon at her, and fired once, twice, a third time.

Two bullets hit the back of the elevator. The third was embedded in one panel of the door's two panels as it finally slid shut.

Twenty-one floors to go!
Twenty!
Nineteen.
Eight—
Suddenly the elevator stopped just before the eighteenth floor. The lights inside—in the ceiling and on the panel of buttons—started flickering, then went out.
Darkness.
Oh God, she prayed. *Oh God, help me!*
Movement.
The elevator shook slightly.
Above!
On the roof. Footsteps. Banging sounds. Something being turned, like a large screw that was noisily loosened. Followed by another. And another.
A brief moment of silence.
And then a sliding panel in the ceiling was lifted away.
Bracing her back against one corner of the elevator, Heather aimed the pistol and fired in that direction.
A gasp of pain.
Another man, quite husky, also wearing a stocking over his face, fell partway through the opening, one arm dangling.
Heather waited to see if he would move. Finally, she slid the pistol into a pocket of her dress and stood before the elevator door. She tried to force it open by pulling the two panels apart, but failed. Nick might have been successful, but she didn't have his strength and stopped trying.
She had only two choices: The first meant staying within the confines of the elevator, while hoping that she would be found. But there was no guarantee that the *right* people would be the ones to find her.
The second choice made her gulp a couple of times.

She could get up on top of the elevator and try to see if any of the doors to the other floors happened to be open. This was unlikely, but then the third man obviously had a way of jumping onto it, and he might have left—

But, first, she had to drag him down from the opening!

At only five feet five inches in height, she couldn't simply stand on her toes, reach up, grab his clothes, and pull, because there was no way she could reach that far. Only that one arm, jutting out through the rectangular hole in the ceiling, was within reach.

Heather grabbed it and started stepping backwards, using as much strength as she was capable of, straining, his body wedged tightly, but she persisted. First the head, then the other arm, and finally, the rest of his body became unstuck, and it fell in a heap on the floor.

She would have to stand on the body before she could reach the opening.

He was on his back. She stepped up onto his chest and stretched her arms above her head, just barely able to close her hands around the edges of the opening as she started to pull herself up.

Heather had managed to get through up to her waist when something strong grabbed first one ankle, then the other.

The man was still alive! He had been only temporarily unconscious.

She kicked back, as hard as she could, and he loosened his grip. She kicked again and was free of him altogether.

As she pulled herself fully on top of the elevator, she saw what he had been doing just before he attempted to get to her. Large, strong screws attaching the elevator car to the cables along which it ran, from the top floor down twenty-eight others to the ground floor, had been loosened and now were nearly all the way out.

The elevator swayed alarmingly.

They wanted to make sure that I was eliminated, she thought. *If any or all of their men failed, then I would be killed this way.*

She inched uncertainly toward the cables.

The elevator made a loud, wrenching sound and moved violently under her feet. She sprang forward and grabbed the cable.

Abruptly, someone screamed a profanity at her. She looked over her shoulder.

The man had pulled himself through the opening, and was lunging toward her. He grabbed her wrist and started pulling at her.

"No!" she screamed at him. "I will not let you throw me in some ditch like you did with my husband!"

He stopped for a moment, looking at her, and, inexplicably, started to laugh.

Heather still had the pistol, and she fumbled for it in her pocket. As she was taking it out, the elevator shook suddenly and broke away from the cable, sliding down the shaft as it began to drop in a free-fall.

Heather hung on to the cable for dear life, but there was a heavy weight—

The man was hanging onto her!

She pressed the barrel of the gun against one shoulder and pulled the trigger. She heard him cry as the bullet tore through him, but he managed to hang on.

Lord, she prayed silently, *please forgive me.*

He was clinging to her as her body strained painfully under

the weight of his own. She brought her arm around to the back of his head.

He tried to stop her, but he had lost too much blood from the original wound and now, rapidly, the one in his shoulder.

Suddenly he looked up at her.

"You don't have to do that," he mumbled hoarsely. "It's all over for me. I know that. But not you, *not at all for you, pretty lady!*

He tried to laugh, but his mouth filled with blood as he let go of her and plunged down into the abyss beneath him.

Heather clung to the cable, wanting to scream but knowing that nobody was around to hear her. She glanced up, hoping to find that one of the doors was open. She saw streams of light penetrating the dark elevator shaft.

Slowly, with great effort, she climbed toward the source. In a short while she was opposite the open door. Now she would have to swing the cable away from the doorway and brace herself as the return motion brought her closer to the edge.

Heather started to do this, the thick heavy steel cable moving with maddening slowness away from and then back toward the open doorway. Preparing to let go of it and leap forward, hopefully with enough momentum to land her on the floor inside, she saw a pair of hands reach out toward her and grab hold. As she struggled, something was being pressed down over her nose and mouth, a sickly sweet stench suffocating her, followed by a darkness so intense that she wondered as it enveloped her if she would ever survive it.

22

★ ★ ★

Heather could sense that someone had spoken to her. She strained whatever faculties she had left in the midst of what seemed certain oblivion.

"You're quite groggy now," the voice said, more clearly now. "That's rather understandable, I must say. Take your time. There's really no rush. My men were able to get you in here before the military could begin its plans to surround and blockade us."

A deep and unpleasant chuckle.

"The military won't attack here as long as we have you," the voice added. "So, we're all safe."

She listened, trying to lock her attention on the voice, using it as a kind of rope to pull her out of her unconsciousness

"You are in for some *very* big surprises, Heather Tazelaar," said the voice, which she now identified as a man's, rather deep, with a guttural edge to it.

Heather attempted to open her eyes but wasn't successful the first time. A minute or so later, her lids parted as she tried again, but there was some pain as she did this, and she immediately closed them.

In the brief flash that got to her pupils before she cut it off, she saw a man on a water bed, his enormous form covering much of it.

Erik Stelzfuss!

"I can't move very well," he went on. "When I do, there is considerable pain. But then that shouldn't surprise you, should it?"

She caught a glimpse of a monstrously heavy man, his clothes on fire, lurching into the surrounding trees, screaming. . . .

Heather tried once more, opened her eyes, saw that she had been propped up on a love seat, her head leaning against a wall with floral-print paper on it.

Stelzfuss's head was turned in her direction.

Special bandages, looking very much like thick strips of flesh, were wrapped around it. She could see only the space around the eyes and the lips.

Grotesque.

She had to turn away.

"Oh, I know," he agreed. "It's quite awful. But Josef is a wizard with skin. He's had practice for half a century."

Heather tried to stand but felt far too dizzy and resigned herself to remaining on the love seat.

"Why did you order my death?" she asked with some nervousness.

Stelzfuss paused.

"Out of revenge for what you have done to me," he replied. "What other reason could there possibly be?"

His manner showed that he was not telling all of the truth, that what he had spoken was only on the surface, nothing deeper.

"There's more," she challenged him. "You were after me well before your car went up into flames."

She thought he had started to grin then.

"You caught me, clever lady," he admitted. "There *is* more, much more, but you shall not learn all of it so easily. Suffice it to say, for the moment, that my order for your execution had to do with the potential for grave trouble that you represented."

"Is that why you had my husband killed?" she asked. "Nick also had become a source for trouble?"

"I was not behind that," replied Stelzfuss, an unreadable, strange tone in his voice. "It was something Josef had been agitating for. I had no interest in the man."

"Mengele wanted Nick dead?"

"That is what he told me. Of course, since your Nick had put so many assorted pieces together, I might well have decided that on my own before long but only as a dispassionate command, something necessary to preserve the secrecy of my, eh, particular kind of business, shall we say."

"Mengele was more emotional about it, more demanding?"

Stelzfuss coughed, then groaned, as he muttered something that sounded like yes.

"But why?" she asked. "Why this one man? Others became aware of the file. What was special about Nick?"

"You are correct, awareness indeed was spreading like some sort of plague," he continued, his voice weaker. "I suppose at some point that I did wonder about Josef's obsession. But after he told me all that your husband was doing, the secrets he had stumbled upon regarding Operation Paperclip, I had no doubt that Nick Tazelaar could not be allowed to remain alive, whoever performed the act."

Heather now struggled to her feet, walked over to a floor-to-ceiling window at the opposite end of the room, and looked out at the beach as foam-crested waves were hitting the shore.

"What about the man in the wheelchair?" she asked, purposely without warning. "And all those photos associated with the Kennedy family?"

Stelzfuss didn't respond.

She waited a minute or two longer and then turned, facing him again.

"Have I touched upon one of your few weak spots, Erik Stelzfuss?" she spoke up angrily. "Are you suddenly remembering perhaps that only your daughter Estelle could have shown them to me?"

She walked over to the bed.

"But then that shouldn't bother you, should it?" she said, her voice rising. "You condemned her mother and grandmother to the hell of Tuskegee and you abandoned your own daughter! Such a man doesn't understand the meaning of—"

She raised a fist, with the intention of hitting that tortured face as hard as she could. His right hand, covered by a leather glove, shot up and grabbed her wrist.

"I kept Estelle *from* Josef," he protested. "I had to choose between the mother and the child. And I—"

His hand dropped back on the bed.

"You're starting to paint a very noble picture of yourself," Heather retorted. "But I'm not buying it. You're the cartel's dictator. You control it. Nobody could force you into any choice. You have been making your own rules for a long time."

He tried to raise his nearly quarter-ton body up on his elbows.

"That is as you say. But every leader, every *boss,* yes, even every tyrant has his enemies waiting to depose him. He has inspired no love, no devotion except out of fear. Loyalty is a will-o'-the-wisp phantom that the slightest breeze will blow away. I can only imagine what these people will do when word of my incapacitation gets around."

Exhausted by just that minimal physical effort, Stelzfuss fell hard against the water-filled mattress, which rolled from side to side.

"I am so weak now," he said. "Please, come closer to me. . . ."

She hesitated, repulsed by the man, by the look of him, by the acts he had perpetrated, by everything that he represented. And yet, as he lay there, his face so pale, his cheeks twitching, his eyes bloodshot, she could feel the slightest thread of pity toward him, pity that ran headlong into her seething hatred and yet somehow survived to draw her closer as he had requested, leaning over him, her ear near his lips.

"I can assure you that Estelle would not have been alive today if I had not sent her as a child out for adoption," he told her in a whispery voice. "The others knew only about her mother because I kept any information about the pregnancy from them. When my daughter was born, I made sure Estelle would be safe, got the best adoption agency to handle the matter . . . while sacrificing the woman who gave birth to her."

"Why couldn't you have kept *both* from harm?" Heather demanded.

"Those in the cartel who would benefit from my downfall had all the names, the number of volunteers for Tuskegee. There would have been no way to explain my wife's disappearance. The victims would have been my child and myself."

"Why did you marry her?"

"Because I loved her."

"Not to have yet another guinea pig for Tuskegee when Estelle was born?"

The bottom edges of the bandages near his eyes were becoming moist.

"Estelle's mother was the only one whose pretense seemed so real. She succeeded in making me believe that this disgusting body was not repulsive to her."

"It is nearly impossible to believe you," confessed Heather. "After all, yours has been the voice that commanded the deaths of countless numbers of helpless people—men, women, and children alike over the years."

A wracking cough shuddered through his frame.

"How can a monster feel any kind of compassion?" he replied after that seizure had stopped. "That is what you think, is it not?"

"Yes. . . ."

"You haven't asked me an obvious question," he told her.

"What's that?"

"Why would I allow Estelle, my child, to continue hating me? Why wouldn't I have attempted to tell her the truth when she was old enough to grasp it?"

"So you *know* that she does carry nothing but this deep hatred for you?"

"I do. . . ."

"That question did occur to me," Heather admitted. "So, what kind of an answer do you have?"

"In hating me, she now wants nothing to do with me. She would prefer to pretend that I don't exist. If she loved me, if she knew I was keeping her out of my life, she might want to see me, to make up for the lost years."

Heather could see that he was narrowing his eyes as he looked intently at her. "And then the others would learn about her. They would do terrible things to my daughter and then dump her on my doorstep while hiding behind their cowardly anonymity."

What he had just told her "connected." Stelzfuss gained nothing by a lie in that instance, so she assumed that he was telling the truth.

Erik Stelzfuss had more to say.

"You mentioned that snapshot of some man in a wheelchair in a room littered with reminders of the Kennedys," he reminded her. "Do this now, Heather Tazelaar. Go next door. That room is unlocked for the moment. There is no guard beside it. Spend some time inside. Then come back to me, and I will clarify for you another example in answer to that question of whether someone such as I can feel any kind of compassion."

23
★ ★ ★

Heather placed her hand on the knob and slowly turned it. The door's hinges squeaked slightly. As she entered, she thought she heard someone grunt, alerted to an intruder by the noise.

The room was perhaps fifteen by twenty feet. Bookshelves lined one wall, framed photographs another, these featuring shots of Caroline Kennedy and John Jr. and Jackie—a large number involving Jackie and Aristotle Onassis.

But she could see others—Marilyn Monroe, dozens of these, quite a few autographed by the actress. Plaques announcing awards for public service were interspersed among the photographs.

And Bobby—from a very young age to one showing him on the floor of the Ambassador Hotel after he had been shot.

Heather turned slowly toward the picture window and the wheelchair in front. There was an odor of waste products in the air. The man obviously had no control of his bodily functions. She could hear him mumbling to himself, those incoherent little sounds uttered by the elderly or the terminally ill, lost in an inner world of pain, despair, and shame over their helplessness.

She had to force herself to walk to his side, to put her hand on the back of the wheelchair, careful not to touch the tubes that fed him nutrients through his arms or the oxygen mask that covered his mouth and his nose.

Slowly, nervous cramps severely twisting her stomach, Heather turned the metal chair around and stepped back for a moment as she saw the man sitting there, his features still visible through the small oxygen mask that had been placed over his nose and mouth. Somehow she was both surprised and yet not surprised by his countenance—both reactions jumbled together as the truth confronted her. He seemed to be looking at her through eyes that had no comprehension, that betrayed no real awareness of his surroundings.

She got down on her knees in front of him and took his hand, which seemed surprisingly firm and youthful, and studied what she could see of that famous face. The hair was as thick as it seemed back in 1963, though much whiter. But the skin had lost its perennial tan and was pale, splotched with little marks, like pimples that had burst and left scars.

And yet . . . she thought as she reached up and touched his right cheek.

Not the face of a man in his seventies! So few wrinkles! Not the leathery look that took over so many of the aged she had seen over the years.

It must be the work of Mengele, she told herself. *He has done something to you, Mr. President, kept at least this outer part of you—*

The lips were moving. A hoarse voice uttered words she could not catch.

"I don't understand," she said. "I don't know what it is that you are trying to say to me, Mr. President."

Tears.

"Are you in pain, sir?" she asked, seeing these as they trickled down the sides of his cheeks.

Again he tried to speak, again the words were unintelligible.

I don't know what it is that you are trying to say to me, Mr. President.

The impact of what she had said stopped any additional words for the moment.

Back in 1963, the world recoiled from the nightmare of John Fitzgerald Kennedy's apparent assassination. And during the thirty years since then, every minute of that twenty-second day of November had been analyzed, examined, and debated, from the events on the grassy knoll to the alleged switching of coffins to the events of a couple of days later, when Jack Ruby murdered Lee Harvey Oswald before so many witnesses, to all the other questions and implications that had surfaced.

And now I kneel before a man who was supposed to be dead and buried three decades ago, Heather thought. *If his death brought about so much uproar, what will the reality of his life cause once the world learns of it?*

She recalled the exploitation stories that surfaced in supermarket tabloids, purported sightings of JFK on an isolated Greek isle and elsewhere, accompanied by grainy, out-of-focus photos that supposedly proved the validity of those reports. She wondered now how many had caught just bits and pieces of the truth amidst all the hokiness and obvious fabrications.

Again and again during her short time in that room, he tried to say something only to have his words destroyed by vocal cords that must have suffered ghastly damage from the bullets that entered his body.

A sheet of paper! The thought hit Heather suddenly.

"Would you write down what you have been trying to say?" she asked. "Would you be able to do that?"

He sat there as before, no expression whatever on his face.

As Heather was standing, she noticed something on his right shoulder, a whitish smudge on the dark blue pajamas he was wearing. She reached out, touched it, and some of whatever it was rubbed off on her fingers.

Dye . . . white dye.

She shrugged and glanced about the room, then saw a crumpled sheet of paper in a bucket near the wheelchair. It took a minute or two longer to find a pencil.

Heather returned to the wheelchair, sat down again in front of it, placed the sheet and the pencil on the still, silent figure's lap, then realized she had forgotten some stiff backing on which to rest the paper.

She got to her feet again, looked once more over what was in that room: a rectangular table to one side, a rocking chair to the left of it, the seventy-inch projection TV set, the Kennedy family photographs, and a small leather-bound book on an end table.

She walked over to the book, saw that it was a diary, picked it up, opened the cover, and read the inscription inside:

> *To my president,*
> *With regret that I could not stop those who sought to take your life. . . .*
>
> *Love,*
> *Erik Stelzfuss*

Stunned, she dropped it on the floor and stood, trembling, the possibility that Stelzfuss, a corrupt and despicable man and a murderer on a mammoth cumulative scale, had *not* been connected with the assassination attempt on John Fitzgerald Kennedy sending a wave of chills throughout her body.

Heather turned toward the door, forgetting the diary and the occupant of that wheelchair, opened the door, wandered from that room back to the one next to it, and entered, to stand before the huge blob of a man who seemed every bit as feeble and tired as the ravaged husk of a once-vital president she had just left.

"Tell me what happened. Tell me only the truth."

"Am I capable of that?" he retorted. "Can you depend upon what I will say?"

"I pray so," she said. "I pray so."

"I have prayed, too," he continued. "I have prayed for death. I almost died that day you caused my limousine to burst into flames. Have you any idea what that kind of searing heat is like? When most people burn a finger on a stove, it is, to them, a terrible thing. But that is pain of only a fleeting nature."

He changed position slightly on top of the water bed. "Just that tiny bit of movement is agony for me, Heather Tazelaar," he acknowledged. "I feel as though my body is a giant blister, and I am encased in it. I live in fear of infection, I live in fear that it will burst and everything I am will drain away, leaving only a shrunken, soggy mess behind, so grotesque that those who cart it away to dispose of it will be sickened by what they witness."

She grimaced as he spoke.

"I can see that that disturbs you," Stelzfuss observed. "But there is more. When I dream, I dream of what you Christians call hell. And it is no different from what I am experiencing now *except that I am being continually burned and the pain never ends!*"

His entire bulk shook as he sobbed from those visions in the night, haunting images that stayed with him well after he would awaken, daylight bringing no relief from them.

She reached out and wiped away a tear that had started to trickle out of the corner of his left eye.

"You mustn't do that," he said, turning away from her. "I deserve no pity whatever, I deserve only the punishment that is mine as I lie here, that my dreams tell me will *be* mine when I leave this life!"

"I agree," she spoke, "but I saw the diary a moment ago. I saw what you had written inside. Tell me what happened. Tell me as much as you are able."

Stelzfuss lapsed into silence, as though to gain a bit of strength. Then he went on to say, "The president alienated many within the military. He wanted to close down the Vietnam conflict. He hoped to stop the nuclear arms race. When he wasn't distracted by an extramarital affair he could think clearly, his instincts as a president far outclassing his questionable loyalties as a husband. But when his mind was on any beautiful woman, the results could be disastrous, as shown by the Bay of Pigs fiasco."

"Are you saying the U.S. military had some connection with the attempted murder of a president?" pressed Heather incredulously.

"I am saying that, and more. Castro had nothing to do with it. But the military establishment did, aided by the mafia. They formed an alliance, and you see, in the next room, what the result was."

"Your inscription said that you tried to stop the assassination but failed. And yet John Kennedy continues to live."

"My operatives switched the coffins," Stelzfuss said simply. "I assigned Mengele the task of making sure that the president survived. Whatever you might think of him, however much of a criminal he is, Josef Mengele also has a certain genius—unhinged and obsessed by bizarre cravings, yes, but genius just the same. Any *normal* surgeon could not have accomplished what he did."

"What if Mengele had failed? What would you have done?"

"I would have had him killed and his body deposited at the Israeli consulate's office in Washington, D.C."

"And today?"

"The warning stands. Mengele and his associates remain alive only as long as that man in the next room does."

"So the story Nick was on the verge of exposing was only partly about the cartel itself then?"

"You are correct. Nick would have died if only the Kennedy chapter, shall we say, had been at risk. I could allow no one to find out that John was alive. Imagine what the media would have done with that story! The tabloids have a field day with mere rumors. What if a living, breathing, John Fitzgerald Kennedy were produced?"

"But what did Marilyn Monroe have to do with it?" she demanded.

"Nothing, obviously, as far as his supposed death was concerned. The problem with Marilyn occurred much earlier. You see, I adored the Kennedys, and they at least tolerated me. I was responsible for getting them most of their women."

Heather stepped back in disgust.

"I know that that offends your Christian sensibilities, but I cannot help that, Heather Tazelaar. They welcomed me into their inner sanctum. Whatever their motivation, they succeeded in making me feel accepted. I didn't have to threaten them. I held no real, direct power over them. I simply helped them indulge their insatiable sexual appetites."

Heather was fighting to control her feelings.

"You haven't answered my question about Marilyn," she managed to say.

"She was going to hurt them, hurt them quite badly," Stelzfuss explained. "I couldn't allow that. I ordered Sambuco to set it up."

"You *ordered* Carmine Sambuco around?"

"He needed me for his guns, for his ammo, for a great deal more than that. He did favors for me from time to time."

"But he was in love with her at one point," Heather reminded Stelzfuss. "How could he do such a thing?"

"For some men, appealing to their wallets has more impact than anything sexual. With that guy, making money, keeping it, and all the power this brought with it was a kind of sensual experience anyway."

"And my Nick stumbled into the midst of all this! You knew how close he was coming to piecing *everything* together."

"That was when Mengele took over. He promised to pursue your husband's annihilation with some gusto. He could hardly wait to get his hands on the man. I thought him excessive at the time, and I still do as I think about it."

"All this to keep a man shielded from public view," she said, "to perpetuate the myth of his death."

"You saw the reason," he added. "The public's image of JFK is one of a vibrant, dynamic individual, a still-young man, a King Arthur extending the boundaries of Camelot. Look at what he has become. He has no control of his bodily functions. A steel plate is embedded in his skull to keep his brain in place. He cannot talk well or for a prolonged period of time because his vocal cords were damaged. Most of the time he cannot talk at all since this requires too much effort and he doesn't have the strength.

"He does little but sit there, drooling out of the corners of his mouth and sometimes, I presume unintentionally, spitting phlegm into the face of anyone who happens to be with him at the moment. People must never see what he is today. They must never know about the past thirty years!"

"But that is simply another deception," Heather argued. "The public was deceived from the beginning. They were *sold* the image you speak of, a fluffy PR concoction that had far less to do with reality than the dozens of women he slept with, *that you obtained for him!*"

She was finding it difficult to keep her temper in check.

"John Fitzgerald Kennedy was the most immoral president in the history of the country!" she declared. "And yet many still place him on a pedestal, before which they stand with their posthumous adoration."

Stelzfuss brought his gloved hands together in a gesture of soundless clapping.

"Well spoken," he remarked. "But you forget one thing."

"What is that?" she spat out the words.

"When you came back here from that room after spending time with him, your face was white, your hands were shaking, and you could barely speak. The man you saw in that wheelchair is old, very sick, physically scarred, a pitiable wreck after all this time. Could *you* make the decision to lift the lid on what has happened and present that poor soul to the world?"

"But I couldn't commit murder in order to maintain the secrecy," she said, evading a direct answer.

"What if it were your precious Nick in that chair instead of the president of the United States?" Stelzfuss probed. "Would your answer be the same, Heather Tazelaar?"

She wanted to give him an emphatic no, spit it in his face, walk out, and leave him behind her without ever turning back.

"You wanted to kill me a short while ago," he persisted, "because of what I *had* done to Nick. I have killed for much the same reason—because of what the gossipmongers, the sensationalists *would* do to that wreck next door if they ever found out about his existence. Your act of violence would be reactive, mine preventative. Otherwise the motivation is identical."

Heather could no longer stand. She threw one hand against the wall in back of her, trying to steady herself.

"I will call Mengele," said Stelzfuss. "He can give you something."

"No! Not him!" she implored. *"Not that devil!"*

Stelzfuss was about to press a button on a control box near his right hand when the door opened and Josef Mengele, the death doctor of Auschwitz, stood just outside in the corridor, looking at the two of them, his face contorted by panic.

"They never intended a blockade, Erik!" he growled. "SWAT teams, Erik. They're on the grounds now. Your guests are furious."

Mengele, appearing every bit his eighty years, stepped forward. He was dressed in surgical garb, an open scalpel protruding from one pocket, a pair of long, sharp surgical scissors from the other.

"I'll kill the woman and then destroy the records," he said. "We've got to hurry. Oh, Erik, we—"

Blindly, in a rage unlike any that had taken hold of her before, Heather jumped to her feet and lunged for Mengele, knocking him to the floor. He closed his old wrinkled fingers around her throat, and his strength surprised her. She grabbed the scalpel, but it was knocked from her hand before she could use it as a weapon.

Heather gasped for air, Mengele on top of her now yelling obscenities. She reached for the scissors, closed her fingers around the handle, and jammed the long blades at him again and again. He tried desperately to stop her but was stabbed in his hand, in his arm, in his leg, yelling with pain and snarling with rage.

But he managed to hold the grip on her throat.

She was nearly unconscious now. She had only one chance and abruptly jabbed upward at his throat, the blades piercing above his Adam's apple and into the soft flesh and muscle just below his jaw.

He stumbled backward, crying out, holding both hands now at his own throat. He looked directly at Heather once, an expression of dark and unholy malevolence on his face, and then collapsed on the floor.

She stood, unsteadily, coughing, her throat muscles badly bruised, and turned back toward the room where Erik Stelzfuss was confined.

"Do you know what you have done, woman?" she could hear Erik Stelzfuss telling her. "He was a madman, but he had some valuable techniques, some skills. Without him, you have doomed me, and you have doomed that pathetic creature next door."

He had lifted himself partway up from the mattress.

"But there comes a point when life should not be pro-longed," he told her, "when death should be allowed its natural course. You may not believe that, but men like me do. When life is so ugly, when it has become nothing but a circle

239

Roger Elwood

of deception, when it no longer has any *justification,* we are inclined toward ending it, with whatever means are at our disposal."

Heather dimly saw him climbing agonizingly out of the bed, the bandages on his face becoming soaked with fluids from bursting blisters, grunts of pain accompanying every movement.

"Please," he begged, "as mad as it may sound, I must ask of you a favor. Go back to my daughter, try to get her to believe that I did love her, that I loved her mother, that I wish her only the greatest happiness for the rest of her life."

He took Heather's hand in his own, with surprising gentleness, and pried the scissors away from her, tossing them to one side on the floor.

"I am sorry for everything," he said, "so very sorry, pretty lady."

And then Erik Stelzfuss turned back toward the bed, gasping as he did so, and seemed to be cupping his hands in front of him while bowing his head.

"I didn't know that you prayed," she said, surprised, but not sarcastic in her tone.

Too late to stop him, Heather saw Stelzfuss put the barrel of a gun in his mouth and pull the trigger, his great bulk collapsing on the floor.

Heather stumbled from the room. She did not notice Lloyd Brahill at the opposite end of the corridor, running toward her. She could see only the two bodies at her feet and think of the old man next door, alone, unaware that he could not now escape being exploited as a sideshow freak, surrounded mostly by the pity of a world that once adored him.

Brahill was at her side now.

"Thank God you're safe," he said, panting.

240

"In there," she spoke up. "He's in there, Lloyd."

"Who, Heather? Who are you talking about?"

She told him.

His hand shaking, he used a two-way radio and ordered immediate help.

"He'll be guarded as no one before in history has been," he said when he finished, his voice trembling.

"Guarded from the cartel, I know. But how can he be protected from the media, Lloyd, from all the people who made him the stuff of legends? And who is going to tell his family? Do you want that job, Lloyd? Could you do that? And then show everyone the enfeebled, moronic husk that is all that is left of him?"

Brahill's shoulders slumped.

"We can't forget that he exists," he argued. "Nor can we just leave him here."

"We can take away his oxygen," she said, hating the thought as soon as it was spoken. "It won't take long, a couple of minutes perhaps. Isn't that better than what he would have to endure if the news got out? He's had thirty years already of this, Lloyd. He may not deserve our admiration as a man, but we cannot inflict more of this punishment on him, this suffering."

She looked at her friend without blinking, and he did likewise with her.

"You cannot do that," Brahill protested. "It goes against what you believe, it violates your faith in a very clear and awful way."

"We can make sure that that room is off-limits until he's dead," Heather added, as though not hearing him, "and then the body bag is simply marked UNIDENTIFIED, and he is buried in an unknown grave somewhere. We can do that, Lloyd, can't we? Wouldn't that be the more merciful thing?"

Tears were draining down Brahill's cheek.

"Yes, we can, we can," he said. "You're right, you're absolutely right. We would be doing him a favor. But . . . but that would be making God's decision for him! Don't you see that? How can *you* advocate this, Heather? We don't have the right."

"Let's go in now, Lloyd," she demanded, still oblivious, still dominated by emotions that she knew she would regret in an hour, a day, longer. "We'll walk in together, and I'll introduce you to him. Then tell me, when you can talk at all, what is right."

She grabbed his hand and half pulled him along with her. The door was still open.

"Mr. Brahill!" a young man waving a file folder through the air was shouting at him halfway down the corridor. "We've found something, something extraordinary."

"Later," Brahill shouted back.

"But, sir, it wasn't Nick Tazelaar's body in that ditch outside Düsseldorf, Germany," the other tried to tell him. "You may not believe this— I scarcely can—but this file says that it was the body of—"

Brahill slammed the door behind him, cutting off the young man's words without hearing anything that he had said.

"Spasms of some sort," Brahill observed.

That frail body shook with some violence for a moment, and thick fluids dribbled over the thin lips and down his chin. Seconds later, he was quiet again.

Forgive me, Lord, Heather prayed as she reached for the oxygen mask, then stopped, seeing this shattered man so helpless, utterly at her mercy, and she knew she could not go on with what seemed an act of mercy just moments before.

"Forgive me, Mr. President," she said with greatest tenderness, "for I cannot do what I thought I must, no matter how much your pain may be now."

A bony hand, with sick, gray-toned veins near the surface, rose up slowly, the fingers closing around her wrist.

"Lloyd!" Heather spoke up. "Lloyd, he's—"

Those beet-red, diseased lips were moving slowly, sounds coming from deep within his throat, and he was shaking his head.

"I can't understand, Mr. President," she told him. "I can't understand what you are trying to tell me."

"He doesn't want to die," Brahill was saying. "He thought you were going to—"

Abruptly, the figure in the wheelchair seemed to be trying to stand. As he did, the strain causing veins to stand out on his forehead, the oxygen mask was torn from his face, and he seemed to be saying something, but his voice was too low, and they couldn't hear what the words were.

Brahill rushed over to him and grabbed his shoulders, gently stopping him from any further movement. He noticed the white dye on that right shoulder. There was more of it now, down the arm itself, and on the front of the pajamas.

Their eyes met. There was now a weak but evident smile on that tortured face.

Brahill leaned over, placing his left ear next to a mouth from which sounds were coming that were somehow more recognizably words than the previously unintelligible noises.

"I'm . . . dying . . . now . . . Lloyd . . . I need to put my arms around her, my dear friend."

243

"How did you know my name?" Brahill blurted out. "How could you—?"

His body was drenched with perspiration in an instant as he realized the stark and powerful truth. Slowly, every muscle reluctant, he rose and turned to Heather, his movements that of a primitive robot, all feeling, all emotion having stopped, for if he allowed himself to feel anything, he knew he would surely collapse.

"Sit down in front of him, Heather," he said mechanically.

"But I can't," she protested, chills racing along her spine, a desire to run from that place almost compelling her to ignore him and leave as quickly as possible. "Without that oxygen mask, I can see him more clearly now. He seems so much like—"

"Do it, Heather," Brahill interrupted, turning away, unable to maintain eye contact any longer. "Be close to him."

She got down on her knees as her friend had asked.

The dying man leaned forward, reached his arms out and wrapped them around her as he whispered, with sudden clarity, "I prayed that the Lord would keep me alive until I could hold you just one more time. . . . *Goodbye now, my beloved.*"

A single gasp came from Nick Tazelaar in that final instant of his life, his body at last freed of pain as it fell forward, limp against her own.

Sliding out of his grasp, Heather leaned him gently back in the wheelchair. She then stumbled from the room. She slid down one wall and sat on the floor, her legs pulled up close to her chest, her head bowed, her body seemingly about to explode as sobs tore through it.

She heard Lloyd Brahill sit beside her, felt his arm on her shoulder.

"It was so awful hearing that he had died," she said, "so hard living without him. And now . . . now . . ."

She looked at Brahill, the words choking in her throat before she managed to thrust them out.

"How can I go on, Lloyd?" she asked. "How can I face this alone?"

"You won't *be* alone," he tried to persuade her.

Suddenly another voice intruded.

"He's right, you know. . . . I'll be there with you."

Heather looked up to find Becky Huizinga walking down the corridor toward her, arms outstretched, tears streaking down her own cheeks.

A moment later, the two women were embracing.

"Don't give up," Becky begged. "Lean on me."

"Nick's here," Heather whispered. "He's—"

Becky placed a finger on Heather's lips.

"I know. Mengele gloatingly let me know about that as well. I kept praying that you would never find out."

"But I did . . . oh, I did! If I had never known, I would not have been able to hold him that . . . that final time."

"It's full cycle, you know," Becky said. "We were together when we first got the news that they supposedly were dead. Now that they really are, it's the two of us again. I don't know what God has in mind, but whatever the case, it is a part of His plan. We have to believe that and accept whatever happens next."

"You've thought it all out?" Heather asked. "Everything's fallen into place?"

"Little of *anything* has fallen into place. I just came to accept what I couldn't change—that Douglas was with the Lord and I was left behind for awhile, and there was nothing, nothing at all I could do about that. I had to place myself totally in His care.

"It was then that I felt a measure of peace . . . not much, Heather, it's nothing other than a tentative starting point, a baby step, I guess, but I'm here, I've got you, and that's the way it is. I wish I could offer you more than this—but it's all I have."

Heather turned toward that one room.

"I . . . I want to go back in there once more," she said. "I want to just sit with him for a few minutes."

"I'll join you," Becky told her. "I mean, if you want me to."

"Yes, I want you with me," Heather replied. "Praise God I have you."

She started to ask Lloyd Brahill if he could wait, but before she had finished the sentence, he was telling her that this was fine.

The two women hesitated as they approached the doorway.

"Go ahead," Becky said, voice cracking. "Sit with Nick. Hold him again. I'll be right with you. Really I will."

Heather nodded, then walked over to the wheelchair, sat down beside it, and held both of his hands.

Finally Becky joined her, and the two of them cried until no more tears would come.